Pride Publishing books by J. Calamy

Diving In
Drifting

I0570354

Diving In

DRIFTING

J CALAMY

Drifting
ISBN # 978-1-80250-992-2
©Copyright J Calamy 2022
Cover Art by Fiona Jayde ©Copyright June 2022
Interior text design by Claire Siemaszkiewicz
Pride Publishing

DRIFTING

Dedication

To my dive buddy, Thad.

Acknowledgements

Susan, whose comment about embassy art displays during a trip to Uganda summoned Cole Hadley like some kind of marshmallow demon.
The group chats, which provided all the support and cheerleading for this work.
My editor Rebecca, who made me use the past perfect participle exclamative.

Chapter One

Cole

It wasn't fair to be this cold on the shores of the Sahara. Despite the broiling heat trying to claw its way through the cracks under the doors, the air conditioning of the Hotel Grande Al'Shahin was arctic, setting Cole's teeth chattering and chilling his clammy shirt to his back. Hugging himself, he didn't catch the concierge's spiel.

"I'm sorry, what?"

"Our pool has a dance show every night at six o'clock." She pressed a stack of brochures into Cole's hands then glanced at his belly...again. He managed not to tug at his shirt this time as her voice dropped into a conspiratorial murmur. "We have the *best* in-house gym, and the spa has an amazing detox wrap. Takes *inches* off. Incredible results."

How delightful. Cole couldn't muster a single response, his mind clicking like a car with a dead battery. None of his canned responses, perfected over the last two years, were coming. Only his therapist's *"You don't always have to educate people. Sometimes it's okay to ignore them."*

"I'm more interested in diving lessons," Cole said, trying not to clench his teeth. "But thank you."

Her face went blank, but not before assuming a brief look of incredulity that didn't help with the teeth clenching at all. "Diving? We have a full-service dive shop," she said. "They do intro classes every Monday, Wednesday and Friday and twice on Saturday. If you…know how to swim?"

"Sounds great," Cole said, sliding away. That was enough BS for one day. The flight from Cairo had been short but brutal — he didn't need this on top.

Despite his grand-sounding title — and the State Department loved titles — as the Assistant Cultural Attaché to the United States Embassy, Cairo, Cole had flown in a middle seat. *On the return flight I'm upgrading. Never letting the morale office book me a flight again.* He'd pretended to be asleep to avoid seeing the faces of his row-mates. Legs and arms clenched tight, seatbelt cutting his hips despite the extension, Cole had barely breathed the whole flight.

The heat and salt marsh air of Al'Shahin had slapped him the moment he'd staggered off the plane onto the shimmering tarmac. Clean air, to be sure, but also hot. Broiling, unbelievably hot. And humid! Trapped against the Sinai, Al'Shahin stewed in the evaporation off the Red Sea. Less than a year in Egypt, and he thought he had mastered the heat. Humidity had not even occurred to him.

Neither had freezing to death in a hotel lobby. It was eleven a.m., and he was exhausted. A backhanded insult about his weight wasn't the welcome he'd imagined. Three years ago, he would have broken down in tears. A year ago, he would have given her a lecture. But present-day Cole shrugged it off, making for the doors. *They always mean well, don't they? And maybe I'll get the fucking wrap anyway. Maybe I wanted to before she even said anything. So there.*

He took a deep breath before pushing out onto the patio. The heat clawed him with greedy fingers, sun blazing cheerfully away overhead. Three steps, and he could feel the heat in his mouth. Five, and he could sense it through the soles of his shoes. The back of his neck burned, and he looked around, trying to shake off the feeling of being watched. Stared at. *You are being paranoid. It's just the heat.*

The pool shimmered, a mirage of blue. Darker sunglasses, they were first on the shopping list. Christ, and he thought Cairo was hot? Still feeling eyes on him, he tried to walk quickly but not too quickly, ignoring the rattle of his suitcase wheels over the pebbled walk. The sweat on his lower back itched. *A shower. A shower and a nap then I can reassess.* Hands slick, he bobbled his phone, dropped it and his sunglasses both. Someone laughed. Cole flinched, even as his brain registered the sound was happy, flirtatious laughter. Not *look at that loser* laughter.

"You are not a loser," he muttered, gripping his phone and straightening his sunglasses. He gave his shirt a sharp tug over his belly. "You have never been a loser. Those were Donnie's words." He hadn't needed that mantra in a while. Cairo was…good. Busy, interesting, professionally validating and really fricking good. Living in a cramped Cairo apartment? Not so much. But who cared? It was Cairo! The geography and antiquities nerd dream.

But now here he was, thinking of his ex, feeling eyes watching him, hurt and slipping into intrusive thoughts. Why? Just because people were laughing?

"All right, all right, quit messing around," a rough voice barked out, making Cole fumble his phone again. The happy laughter cut off in a chorus of groans. "I don't *care* how tired you are! You clean your gear, then you can relax."

A small building squatted on the far side of the pool, with a thatch roof and an open central arcade, shaded and tiled in blue. The dive shop. The sign over the opening was faded, a shark curled dimly under the Grande logo. One of the million old pickup trucks littering Africa was backed up to the arcade, and a group of young people passed equipment back and forth like hurrying ants.

The bark belonged to a tall, scowling man standing in the bed of the truck with his hands on his hips and glaring straight at Cole from behind a pair of mirrored aviators.

Tanned from the sun, with wide shoulders, he wore a wetsuit unzipped to the waist and hanging around his legs. He had a shaved head and short scruffy beard, brown heavily threaded with gray. The harsh lines of his face made art deco angles with his jaw as he shouted at the divers scrambling around the truck. Whoever this pissed-off jerk thought he was, he was staring at Cole.

Taking a slow deep-oven-hot breath, Cole straightened his sunglasses, glancing back over out of the corner of his eye. His championship record of making a fool of himself in front of hot straight men made him cautious, but he didn't miss the way the guy in the truck glanced his way again. Busted.

"It ain't complicated, doll." The divemaster sneered at a pretty blonde girl with her hands on her hips. "You rinse the salt off *your* gear, *you* hang it up, and then you can eat."

What an absolute dick. Cole knew trouble when he saw it. Hopefully that guy wouldn't be the divemaster for Cole's certification. Cole was in no mood. He kept walking.

His room was one in a long row of little villas. Did a one-bedroom with en-suite count as a villa? The brochure certainly said it did. And for Cole, who only intended to use the room to sleep after days of adventure, it was pure luxury. A quick walk-through revealed air conditioning, a huge bed piled high with blue pillows and a tiny bathroom. Bright and cheerful, it was certainly bigger than his airless shoebox in Cairo.

The back door opened onto a small limestone courtyard, high walled and full of plants. The back of the house blocked the blazing sun. Stepping onto the tiles, Cole gave a whoop of joy, seeing an outdoor shower, the showerhead as big as a tennis racket. Cole had no trouble ignoring the rust and the slightly crooked pipes. He turned on the water and after some screeching rattles, it gushed a monsoon. Cole needed no further prompting. He stripped right there, laying his clothes on the shelf by the towels and toiletries.

"*Heaven.*"

The blue sky, the reaching plants, the patter of water on the stones... Cole took the first relaxed breath of his leave. Shampooing absently, he realized the sound that had been in the background wasn't air-con—it was the sea!

I'm here! I'm on the Red Sea! The Sinai! Six years in that dank basement office at Smithsonian, trying to get a Foreign Service posting, and now I'm on the Red Sea!

So why was he so jittery? Letting the water flow over him, cooling his sweat-itch skin, he took a moment to assess. Why had the hotel clerk bothered him so much? To the point that he'd nearly had an anxiety attack by the pool?

"I am tired as hell," he said. "I worked like crazy to be able to take a whole two weeks." *Not enough sleep. What else?* "I'm hungry. I missed dinner, and only had airplane coffee." It made more sense when he thought in those terms. His therapist always insisted he run through basic logistics as a first step to challenging negative thoughts. Hungry, dehydrated, sleep deprived, not enough time outside — these were all things that had to be taken care of before he could work on emotions.

"Three triggers at *least* didn't help." Flying was always difficult for him. Then the clerk. Then the mean-faced guy staring at him. His reactions put into perspective, he could finally loosen his shoulders. Relief and gratitude, those glorious balms, filled him as he took three breaths in then gave a long slow exhale, over and over, rocking side to side under the water. *Better. Much better.*

Running soapy hands over himself felt taboo under the open sky. He gave a brief thought to the big scuba instructor by the pool. *He was hot and probably wasn't staring. Thinking about Donnie threw me off.* Three years, give or take, since the divorce, and Cole sometimes went a whole month without thinking about his ex. This seemed like the perfect place to continue that trend.

"I am about to cross something off my bucket list. This is going to be the best vacation of my life, and I am sure as shit not letting *him* spoil even a minute of it."

Him could be Donnie or could be the mean-faced divemaster. Either way. Under the blue sky with the sea calling? Cole's spirits soared. This trip was about adventure, and he was not wasting any of it.

After a bottle of water and a protein bar from his bag, Cole didn't need a nap. He was ready to explore. He threw on clean clothes and, grabbing a hat this time, headed back out to the patio. He wanted to see the water. A whole year in country before his first vacation, he hadn't seen the Red Sea since he'd arrived in Cairo. He tucked his dive paperwork into his back pocket. Since his path took him by the dive shop, he would sign up while he was there. Adventure was calling!

A cascade of wide sandstone steps led to the sea. Umbrellas and chairs dotted the beach in neat rows, broken up by a large bar with a thatch roof. A jetty divided the beach and led straight out into the blue. Nearer shore were a mix of reef and sandy stretches where people could swim and snorkel. *Could* swim. But were not currently swimming. Only one couple used the chaises. A family peered at the reef from the end of the jetty, their voices echoing off the stone walls. The rest of the sandy spar was deserted. Even up on the pool deck, there were only a handful of people. A man sunbathed with an armed bodyguard standing discreetly apart, watching everyone, though there was no one to watch besides some college kids and an elderly couple. Tinny music played over speakers mounted to the dusty palm trees. It echoed strangely, cheerful in the near silence.

The Regional Security Chief had warned him about this. *"You'll get a great deal — you can stay in a really big resort for the cost of those little places a couple years ago. They're in a hard patch. Arab Spring, then the terrorist attacks a couple of years ago, and the economy tanking — there is a lot less business. It's a great time to go. But I worry about those guys. Tourism is everything and that coast is a gem."*

The Chief had been right. Spread out before Cole was a perfect deep blue sea, surrounded by red and brown mountains dropping all the way down into the water. The waves were small, crashing against the reef rather than the moon sliver of sand. Overhead, a wavering dome of white-blue barely tinged to pink as the sun arced to the mountains behind him. Cole did a slow turn, wonder bubbling up. The resort was an oasis of carefully cultivated green cupped in the barren hills, dotted with clean rows of white buildings, his own little villa among them. A gem.

Was this much happiness possible? Physiologically speaking? Would he burst into flames? He had a sense that just out of his peripheral vision, or maybe just beyond his fingertips, was a new stage of his life. If he turned, or reached for it, it would disappear. It danced on the tip of his tongue. *Laura said I needed to fill my well.* Despite the torrent of jokes that followed about what he could fill his well with, she'd had a point. *I'll never paint again if I don't slow down.*

That might be what he was feeling, the itch in his fingers, the change standing just behind him. Maybe it was a muse. The headlong rush into the foreign service was done. He was settled. It was time to breathe. To be still long enough for his muse to find him.

Chapter Two

Hank

Hank Ashton straightened his shirt before knocking on Samir's door. His shirt was the uniform polo—everyone who worked at the Al'Shahin Grande had a closet-full. Blue, the white logo on the breast with *Divemaster* underneath in neat serif, Hank's was still crisp and dark. After all, he spent most of his working hours in a wetsuit. The hotel shirt got him through the gates, down the path to the shop, where he hung it up in the employee changing room, not putting it back on again until it was time to go home. It was immaculate. He tugged at the collar, trying to get it to sit comfortably…a pointless exercise.

"Sit, Hank," Samir said, without looking up. Spots danced as Hank rubbed his grainy eyes. He was bone-tired. And he had three more days? *Christ.* Knowing there was no point in starting a conversation, Hank stared out of the window over Samir's shoulder. The cool dark of the arcade, stripe of blinding white wall and deep blue sea was a static print, making no sense to Hank's addled senses. The illusion was broken when a gull, shouting to its friends, soared across the blue. The image snapped into focus, the fore, middle and background clear. He saw his reflection in the glass now and dragged a hand over his beard.

When did it get so gray? Shit. You need –

"…sleep!" Samir leaned forward, hands folded on his desk, face in an angry scowl.

"Sorry, what?"

"Are you even listening? Are you sick? What is wrong with you? I got another complaint! We have exactly ten guests and somehow you manage to get two of them to complain to me?" Samir jabbed his finger onto the papers in front of him. "You man the desk today. Joe can take the afternoon class. Take tomorrow off. You need sleep. Get laid. Something. But we cannot afford even one bad TripCounselor review! Not even one, in these times!"

He went on, the usual lecture about the reputation of the Grande, about the importance of their name, of their brand. All things Samir had picked up in the hospitality classes he took at night. Hank had a lot of respect for Samir. But the Grande had not been…well, Grande…in over a decade. Even before the economy tanked, it had been eclipsed by the big chains. The old girl was dying. And Hank, despite his dependence on the job, on Samir's continued benevolence, couldn't help but be glad. *Let the old bitch die. She needs rest as much as I do.*

"Wipe that look off your face," Samir growled. "I know what you are thinking."

"I don't know what you mean."

"You still owe my brother fifteen thousand dollars, Hank Ashton." Samir sat back. "I am not unsympathetic. But you must see the position we are in. We need these reviews. We need happy guests." Samir's face lost some of its edge. "Come on, Hank. There is only so much I can cover for you."

Did Hank deserve a friend like Sam? Doubtful. A good man, but their friendship had suffered over the last few years. *He's my boss. And I owe him.* Guilt twined between them now, replacing the carefree partying of their early years. Sam's hair was pretty damn gray too.

"You're right," Hank sighed. "I'll apologize to the young lady. I should have gone to bed a lot earlier."

"I am worried about you." Samir, earnest-faced, rode right over Hank's protests. "No, listen! You have been changing, brother. No one sees you these days. You don't come and smoke, or play with the kids. My mother, my wife, even my mistress complains. What you need is a —" He leaned forward, lowering his voice though they were in his office in a deserted building. "A man. Go to Sharm, or Tel Aviv —"

"Tel Aviv? How? Khaled has my passport," Hank snapped. He pushed to his feet. He didn't want to hear any more of this. He'd get more grief later in the week from Leila. But their concern only made the rut deeper. He couldn't face it now. "I'm going to log dives. Every dollar counts."

"Listen," Samir said. "I am not my brother. He is a gangster, and an asshole — this I understand. Log today's dives, then go home early. I will sign you out later. You are the best divemaster on the coast, Hank. I need you in top form."

Hank stood, gratitude loosening his shoulders.

"Thanks, Sam," he said. "I'll be in tip-top shape for tomorrow."

"If anyone signs up," Samir said, shaking his head.

"Inshallah," Hank said.

"Inshallah," Samir agreed.

* * * *

In the arcade, cool tile under his feet, Hank settled himself behind the welcome counter and fired up their ancient laptop to log today's dives. It wasn't complicated. He'd done it thousands of times. A bottle of water helped. After a moment he felt sweat on the back of his neck. *Dehydrated? After barking at those kids all day to drink water?* He was slipping, getting old.

He was entering the last details, depth, bottom time, safety stops, when a shadow blocked the end of the arcade. He looked up, forcing his customer-service face into place, chiding himself to do better. It was one thing to be in a rut and another to drag other people down with him.

I'll make Sam's wife an almond cake. That will — Oh. Oh no.

The man standing a few meters away from the counter, shifting from foot to foot, was the one Hank had spotted crossing the patio when he'd got back. Spotted and had tried not to stare at. Now he straightened, tugged his shirt straight, and fought down the wings flapping in his belly.

God, he is so fucking cute. Damn it, damn it. Be cool. Remember where you are.

"Hello?"

"Hi," Hank said. It came out something like a choking cat and even when he managed to turn it into a cough, he caught the other man's snort of laughter. "I mean, uh, sorry. Hi. Welcome to Grande Diving. What can I do for you?" *Rub your back? Suck your – shut up, Hank. Jesus fucking Christ!*

His thoughts were rocketing around loose in his skull, and he forced himself to breathe, keeping his customer-service smile on his face by the skin of his teeth. The man came closer, his smile wide and friendly. A guileless sunshine face complete with dimple and a little gap in his teeth. Round. Everything was round. He had cheeks Hank wanted to squeeze, round pecs and a round belly and round little ears like a bear, to match his dark hair. *A bear. That's the trouble. He looks like a teddy bear.*

"I'm Cole Hadley," the teddy bear said, holding out his hand. Hank managed to shake it for exactly the correct length of time, though he knew his smile bordered on frantic at this point. He couldn't help it. "I'm interested in getting certified. I already did my classroom requirements."

"I'm Hank." Another squawk, and Hank cleared his throat. A deep breath, and he tried again. "I'm the divemaster here. You sound American. Where're you from?"

"I'm from the States but I live here now."

"Oh?" Hank perked up. Perked up like a kid hearing the ice cream truck. *Here? He lives here?* And why did it matter where the teddy bear lived? It would change nothing. *'Cept I might have someone to talk to while I do my time.* Wishful thinking, tottering on an entire tower of wobbly 'if's'. *If he's into dudes, if he's single, if he likes me, if he doesn't mind sneaking around. If if if...*

"In Cairo," Cole said, yanking the bottom 'if' out from Hank's tower. "I did my pool dives there, divemaster signed off."

Hank tried to hide his disappointment. Cairo was six hours away, and he didn't own a car. He could get to Israel faster, back when he'd had a passport and credit cards. The gray clouds closed in again.

"You live here?" Cole continued.

"Unfortunately," Hank said. "I've lived here, oh...I guess about six years now."

"Unfortunately?" The teddy bear cocked his head, and Hank forced his three braincells into line.

"Never you mind. I'm just messin'." *And wouldn't Samir be delighted to hear me bitchin'.*

"You're from the south?"

"North Carolina. You?"

"Delaware."

"Nice to meet you, Cole." Hank's voice didn't crack this time, though his heart was rattling away like a loose bearing. He wanted to warm his hands on Cole's smile, just curl right up under that smile and bask. *Stop looking at his smile. What the hell is coming over you? How desperate for company can you be? Drink water, dumbass, before you get the Grande a lawsuit and have to work off your debt at some tourist camel ride place in Giza.*

"Nice to meet you too." Cole looked at him expectantly, still smiling that ray-of-sunshine grin. There was a pause, as awkward as any in the history of the world, until Hank realized the ball was in his court.

"Ah yeah! Right! Okay," he said, taking the paperwork the teddy bear gave him. Cole having already completed his classwork and pool time meant they could cut straight to the dives. "So you're gonna get your open water cert. Okay, I can do that."

He could almost see Leila shaking her head at him. *Almost fifty years old and acting like this?* Doing stupid things and regretting them had been the central theme of his younger years. *Hell, ain't even been six years ago I sank a whole boat, full of gear, then borrowed money from a crook to cover the cost.* He'd like to think he was wiser now.

"So…just you?" Hank kept his eyes on the paperwork, the back of his neck an inferno.

"Just me." Cole's reply had a brittle edge to it, so Hank forced himself to take a deep slow breath. *None of your business. Lawsuit, remember?*

He was saved by the return of the group from earlier. "Excuse me," Hank murmured. "I gotta give these people back their logs."

"Sure," Cole said. He pulled out his phone and started clicking away while Hank gathered up the group's logbooks. He steeled himself as he approached them. *Is anyone more intimidating than a twenty-year-old Israeli girl with her arms crossed like that? I hope she's the forgiving kind. I gotta make this right or I'm in trouble.*

"Here you go," he said. "And listen, I am really sorry about earlier."

"Don't bother," the blonde said. "We already spoke to your manager."

"It turns out while I was telling you all to drink water, I didn't drink enough myself," Hank said with a shrug. "I have no excuse for being so rude, but I wanted you to know it isn't my usual MO."

The other kids with her seemed mollified, willing to have a little laugh at his expense. The blonde wasn't buying it.

"That's not what I heard," she said. "I asked my friend who came here last month, and she said you were a right son of a bitch." She said *son of a bitch* in Hebrew, but like most people who lived and worked on the Red Sea, Hank knew enough Hebrew, Arabic and French to get by. He sighed. She was right.

"Mitztaeret," he said. What else could he do but apologize? "I mean it, you kids came all this way... Tomorrow's dives are on me, okay?"

"Apology accepted," Blondie said, reluctant but polite.

The brunette reached out and patted his arm. "Go eat something," she said. "I am impossible when I'm hungry. And we missed lunch by going to that wall."

He found himself giving her a real smile. She was right. There was no denying it.

"It was worth it though," the blonde conceded with a sigh. "That turtle..."

"I noted her in your logs," Hank said, pointing to the right page. "You should always add little details like that, to remind you. Not just the time and depth and things. Even that you missed lunch."

"Unlike *that* guy," a boy in the group muttered. They collapsed in giggles. Hank shot a glance over at Cole and saw him staring forward, stiff with embarrassment, his little bear ears red. Hank's smile died.

"Until tomorrow," he said, his teeth clenched around a host of unsaid words.

"Tomorrow we will pack extra lunch," the blonde said.

"If *he's* coming, we will have to," the boy said with a snort.

Hank let the words push him faster to Cole's end of the counter. He wanted to say a thousand reassuring things. But Cole was a man, not some twenty-year-old. And the brittle dignity on his face left no room for platitudes. That being said, the idea of Cole having to spend five days learning to dive with that crew?

Not if I have anything to say about it.

Chapter Three

Cole

Cole held very still. The washes of anger and shame were as familiar as the rising and setting of the sun. He had learned, the hard way, to let them slosh around, making him hot and cold by turn, his emotions scattering everywhere. What was important was the here and now, and letting those feelings just pass on through so he could get on with his life. His new life.

He was not letting things like this run him sideways anymore. *Especially from a handful of Tel Aviv kids who have never met me in their lives. I'm an adult with my own life. A new amazing life. I'm the Deputy Cultural Attaché with the US State Department, no fucking less.*

Hank was back. Gorgeous, muscular, slab-of-granite Hank, with his fake smile and his real scowl and his awful tattoos and shaved head and hot Dad beard. The divemaster looked Cole up and down from behind his shades, drumming his wide, scarred fingers on the counter.

"Are you serious?" he asked. Cole's back stiffened. There were slights he could ignore, but he was well past his limits and getting insulted by some pile of bricks was not happening on this day. Not this year. Not this Cole.

"Excuse me?" he snapped, channeling his best staff meeting voice. "What is that supposed to mean?"

"About diving?" Hank asked, jerking off the shades. "I mean are you serious about diving. Is this just curiosity or —?"

"Oh!" Cole shook out his shoulders, loosened his death grip on the counter. "I'm sorry. I didn't understand. Yes. I am very serious. This is bucket list for me and..." He paused, considering what to say. Hank's face was still closed off but something in his eyes made Cole reconsider.

"I'm an artist," he blurted. "And the ocean has always been really important to me. I'm from the eastern shore. Grew up in the water."

Hank's demeanor changed. It changed right in front of Cole's gaze. A slow smile lit his entire face, his teeth flashing in the dim light. *He has such pretty hazel eyes for an angry bastard. I feel like they should be ice blue or some cliché. Too warm for his personality.* The change was clear — some part of what Cole had said made Hank happy. Happy in a way he had not been until this moment.

"Can I talk you into private lessons?" Hank asked. The counter creaked alarmingly under his forward lean.

"Why?" This pile of bricks had gone from mean guy to eager excitement in a flash. Cole leaned back. "I just need my open water dives."

"Do you really want to learn with them?" Hank said, shooting a glance the way the university kids had gone. "They are not serious. They don't give two fucks about anything."

"You don't know that about them," Cole said, wagging a finger. He leaned forward gingerly, drawn in by Hank's excitement. The counter creaked the other way.

"True. But they're kids," Hank said, rolling his eyes. "Kids who might figure out what they are serious about eventually, but not this week. Not in this class."

"Hey, go easy on the kids. We were all young and clueless, once." Cole wasn't sure why he was defending them, but it was true. He was glad he did when Hank rested his chin on his hand, head tilted like a Labrador. It felt good, to have someone's complete attention this way.

"You ain't even mad?"

"Nah. I have a whole life, a world I love. Who are they? Just random strangers. I bet you ten bucks we'd be best friends by the end of the first day. But why private lessons?"

"If it's about the money —"

"No." Cole laughed, considering his stuffed bank account. The account of a man whose only hobbies were books and pottery, a man who ate street food and bought street art and didn't bother with expensive clothes or anything else. *Someone who hasn't taken a day off in two years.* He had enough per diem socked away to splurge a little. And if the sexy divemaster turned out to be a genuine asshole, Cole would just cancel. The group chat he shared with his best friends from the State Department would be hysterical all the same. Laura and Elia would love this.

"Okay," he said. "Let's give it a shot."

"Good."

The moment drew out again, excitement warm and fluttering in Cole's belly. *It's going to happen. I am getting my open water certification. I'll be a certified diver. And I'm doing my open water in one of the most famous coral reef systems in the world.*

"Hank!" The voice made them both jump. A tall thin man in a matching polo came out of a back office with some papers. He bustled over, smiling widely to Cole.

"Welcome, sir!" he said. "I can take it from here. Hank, why don't you go home?"

Hank's demeanor changed again. Big as he was, he hunched down over Cole's paperwork, looked uneasy for a flash, then his face closed into the scowl Cole now recognized as his default.

"I'm signing this guest up for lessons," he said. "Then I'll go."

There was a brief contest of wills, but Hank simply turned his back and began typing rapidly at the computer. Cole made himself busy on his phone, since staring at Hank's back, stretching his tight polo, seemed unwise in front of his boss? *It has to be his boss.*

"Be here at seven. We'll get you geared up then head to the pool," Hank said over his shoulder.

"So early?"

"I am sure we can accommodate—" the other man said, but Hank shook his head, his shoulders set in a stubborn bunch.

"Seven. That way you won't lose the rest of your day. There are some good tours..." He trailed off, shooting a glance at his boss.

Cole felt like he was watching mental tennis. The boss with his plastered smile covering his frustration, and Hank looking more and more like a boulder, unmovable, arms crossed, feet up on the rungs of the stool. Cole lost it. He burst out laughing, startling both men into looking at him.

"I'll be here at seven," he said. "See you then."

After a slow circuit of the property, and a leisurely snorkel around the deserted pier, Cole decided to order some room service and call his friends. Hank the hunk. Or Hank the Grump King, however Cole was calling him, filled his thoughts in a way that needed some ground-truthing. And for that he needed his friends. He looked at the clock by his bedside and did some quick math, wondering if both Laura, who was in DC, and Elia, currently in Myanmar, could be on at the same time. Barely.

A few chirping dial tones later and the split screen on his laptop showed his two best friends from State, their voices ventriloquist strange with the delay.

"Cole, where are you?" Laura's face swung close to the camera, her curls flopping over her eyes. She was in bed, the glow of her phone casting a blue circle of light on her face.

"I'm on leave in a town called Al'Shahin and it's hot as hell here," Cole said, fighting the urge to shout, like that would help them hear him.

"I'm so jealous! It's cold as heck here!"

"It's hotter than Cairo but the air is clean," Cole said.

Elia's internet caught up, and she shouted right over them, her image wobbling as she walked. Her black hair was in a bun on her head, held by a pen, and her heels click-clacked on tile. "Cole, I saw your article!" she said. "Are the Brits furious?"

"What article?" Laura asked. "And where are you at this hour?"

"I wrote a policy paper on how the Brits need to give back the stuff they *stole* from Egypt," Cole said, letting his pride show through. "And it got into the papers."

Both women on the screen gave thumbs-up.

"I'm just getting into the office," Elia said. "Ambassador Jenks was smug as hell—added it to *all* the weekly highlights briefs! It got picked up by *The Times*! The antiquities director at Smithsonian is furious with you."

"I don't work for him anymore," Cole said with a shrug. "He kept me in the sub-basement for a reason. But Ambassador Jenks pushed me to publish, so fuck Smithsonian."

"I'm proud of you," Laura said with a yawn. "You put up with so much there."

"How is the Red Sea?" Elia asked.

"Hot!" Cole fell forward onto his bed, propped on his elbows "Hotter than a hot place in a hot season with the heat on hot. But it's beautiful. You know what? I don't want to jinx anything, but I think I'll be painting again. There's a really active artist community here. I am going into town for dinner and see if I can meet some artists. Not just for work this time."

"That would be pure triumph!"

"But there is a problem," Cole said. "I signed up for dive lessons to get my cert."

"You can finally join me!" Laura said, rolling sideways in a nest of pillows.

"And the divemaster is like a wall," Cole continued.

Both women had the same reaction, hands thrown up and groans of laughter.

"He is like a giant brick wall man."

"And we were doing so well," Elia said, stirring her coffee.

Laura sat up and pulled the blankets around her. "I approve," she said. "Please go hit that wall, Cole. You have all of my blessings."

"Like a wrecking ball," Elia muttered.

"Nah—he's hot, but kind of an ass," Cole said. "He was yelling at his students and he has that perma-scowl."

Laura was not impressed. "Eff his personality. What you need is some D. I wouldn't say you've been in a rut but..."

"She speaks truth, tragically," Elia said.

Cole gave a mock gasp, clutching imaginary pearls. "How dare you," he said. "First of all, I am here to improve myself."

"Growth," Elia agreed.

"I don't need a brick wall man who doesn't smile and wears a wetsuit for work."

"Cole does not and will not!" Elia said, redoing her bun.

"Well of course you don't need him," Laura said. "But I'm not talking about a relationship. Just a little sword fighting, A little parry, a little thrust... I feel like that would be a great improvement."

Cole couldn't deny that much. *When was the last time I got laid? Back in DC, right before I left. That guy from Fifth Column.*

"I hate when she has a point and makes it," Elia said.

Laura shrugged, holding out her hands like it was her burden to be right. Which it was.

Cole groaned, shaking his head. "That is not the improvement my bullet journal demands," he said. "I'm supposed to be working on my inner peace, not his inner piece."

This brilliant play on words was met with silence. "I made a joke! Jot that down, bitches."

"You should be jotting down your dive instructor's personal information," Laura said.

Elia's screen went blank for a moment, though Cole could still hear her tapping away. When she re-appeared, an image of Hank popped up in the text chat.

"I'm on the website. Is this him?"

"In all his glory. I guess he really is that hot," Cole sighed. Damn it all, there was no escaping it. Hank in aviators at the helm of a boat, all chiseled jaw and bad tattoos…

"Oh my God," Laura said. "Okay, well now you have to fuck him. For all of us."

"On behalf of the American people," Elia agreed.

"A public service," Elia said. "You are a public servant, after all."

Cole gave them a mock salute. "He offered private lessons, and I said yes." He paused a moment. "That sounds bad. I realize now that sounds bad."

"It sure does," Laura said. "I'm so proud."

"Well, it isn't as bad as it sounds," Cole said. "I think the younger students just irritate him. No funny business. I am improving myself."

"We are proud of you," Elia said. "Suspicious, but proud. I have to go do some real work now. Until later, bitches, and send us photos!"

"I'm out too. I'm heading into town tonight," Cole said. "There are some sculptors here that work with alabaster. If I meet them, I'll send you some shots of their work."

Chapter Four

Hank

Hank and Samir watched Cole leave, the teddy bear shaking his head and— Was he laughing at them? Hank loosened his shoulders, caught the smile trying to escape and killed it.

"Hank," Samir said in a low angry voice.

"What?"

"You cannot."

"Can't what?"

"I see you look at him," Samir said. He grabbed Hank's shoulder and shook it, hard. "Remember where we are."

Hank gave Samir a wry look. *Talk about hypocrisy? You and me at the Dancing Crab chasing that hairy British guy?* "You looked at him too!"

"I have a wife and two children to hide behind. But more important than all of this. He is a guest, and my brother is looking for a reason to call in his debt and set you to work in his real business. My influence is limited. Best luck—he forgets about you, lets you work for me. Worst—he hears you fucked around with a guest and—"

Hank looked at his hands. Samir's brother, Khaled, was a gangster. He was involved in any number of unsavory businesses, but Samir meant smuggling. Antiquities, forgeries, stolen goods—Khaled had schemes everywhere. If Hank ever fell behind on his debt, or gave Khaled any excuse, he'd be diving the mud in the Nile, fighting crocodiles for pottery chips and smuggling them into the States.

"Okay, okay," Hank said regretfully. "You're right. I'll be good. And hey, private lessons. That's three times my usual fee—I'll be ahead a month!"

"Good man," Samir said. "Pay off my brother, and you will be back in North Carolina diving for shark teeth and fucking all the fat boys you want."

"He's not just fat, he's—" Hank began.

Samir smacked the back of his head. "He is nothing! Stop thinking about him, immediately!"

"Yeah, yeah. Okay."

Easier said than done. It wasn't that good-looking men didn't come through the Grande. But someone like Cole? An artist. Traveling solo. With a belly Hank wanted to squeeze?

Stop thinking about him?

Impossible.

* * * *

Even if he couldn't afford to eat there, Hank loved walking along the beachside markets. It was a tourist trap, he knew that. But the hanging lights, the hawkers at the doors of the restaurants, the displays of seafood packed on ice, the shops selling every possible version of Horus falcons, scarabs and eyes of Ra, were lively and helped push back the loneliness a little. He usually went late, when the few remaining tourists, exhausted by their trips into the desert or under the waves, were winding down.

The locals rarely appeared before nine or ten. The stalls closed, and the fish were packed up. Locals sat in gendered groups on the restaurant patios, leaning on colorful cushions, smoking tobacco, drinking tea and dishing on news and gossip. An older crowd — the young had scattered to jobs in the cities. But with the tourists stumbling to bed, the artists and poets and fishermen smoked and talked late into the night.

Nods and the occasional friendly wave greeted Hank as he walked. Al'Shahin was a small town, Bohemian, and eccentric enough to embrace an awkward American. They knew he didn't like to talk, though he would sometimes sit and listen, absorbing the mix of Egyptian Arabic, Hebrew, French — all the languages of the Sea. The men had stopped bothering him about family and the women had — mostly — given up matching him with their daughters. He was left alone.

Usually that was all right. But tonight he stalked like a leopard in a cage, rather than his usual aimless stroll. Something dug at him, something like a grain of sand under his skin, an irritant making him rub his sternum and grind his teeth.

Shouts of laughter tripped his headlong stride, a familiar voice among them. Peering around a pillar, Hank saw him. Cole. The teddy bear sat with a circle of locals, his thick, stocky legs crossed under him on the cushion, laughing full out, face red, one hand over his eyes and the other on the shoulder of Nader, who owned the tobacco shop at the end of the road. One of the men was telling an elaborate story, waving his sandal. It had the group howling with laughter.

Hank leaned on the wall of a shuttered T-shirt shop. The grain of sand grew bigger, ground a little harder under his skin. He rubbed his cheeks, fighting off the contagion of laughter bubbling in his chest.

Cole, his Arabic choppy, asked a question— immediately answered by the other men, arguments breaking out that he joined without fear. His comfort was obvious, his grin a beacon dragging Hank forward. No. He planted his feet. *Absolutely not. First of all, he ain't local. Cairo might as well be Mars for all the times I go. Second of all, he's a resort guest. I would lose my job if—*

Hank stiffened. If what? If he went and sat with the group? He and Nader had known each other for five years—so what stopped him? What, exactly, would lose him his job? *Kissing him. Kissing him, running my fingers through that soft hair on his chest. Seeing if his cock is as big as it looked in those trunks. Kissing him. Kissing him for hours. God, when was the last time I kissed someone? I miss that shit. This is too stupid. This is way too stupid.*

Hank peeled himself off the wall, gave one last look and stalked off, rubbing hard at the strange irritant under his sternum.

* * * *

Seeing Cole drag himself into the dive shop the next morning, Hank felt a brief moment of petty happiness. *Go out drinking, having fun, laughing with people—I bet you feel like crap now.* It passed quickly, and in any case, there was nothing for his schadenfreude to catch onto.

Despite his splotchy face, his hair sticking in every direction and his clutched coffee, Cole beamed at Hank. And that smile was... Well it was hard to be petty about.

"Morning, sir. I hope you slept well."

"Sir? Please, call me Cole. And I'm so glad you made me get up! Look at the dawn on the water!" He gave a happy sigh, shading his eyes and sipping his coffee.

Hank squinted at the sea. There were a few pink clouds and the sun, barely clearing the horizon, sent perfect blades of white between them. Each wave had a perfect little moon sliver of gold on its back, and the blue shadows shimmered like a school of fish. Hank slowed, coming to stand by Cole. The wind curled over his scalp and he caught a whiff of soap and sweat from Cole, a sleepy mammalian smell that made it hard to think straight.

"I never noticed," Hank said. The sun rose enough, and the effect was lost, breaking the spell. "You said you were an artist?"

"I suppose." Cole shrugged. "But honestly I haven't made any art in years. Just sort of...blocked?"

"That's too bad," Hank said. "How do you fix something like that?"

"You really can't. I'm trying to be patient with myself about it. At my real job I curate art for the Embassy—finding new artists and getting them exposure. It's a great feeling, but not quite the same. But maybe..." Cole squinted back to the hills behind them. "This place is giving me a feeling. Like maybe I might try to draw a little. See what happens."

Hank filed that information away. He was too distracted by Cole's proximity to focus on it now. Cole was swallowed in a huge T-shirt, but his short, thick legs and wide forearms were enough of a distraction. Hank was a big guy — he swam all day — his physique all hard, narrow edges. Was that why he was so attracted to the opposite? Cole was like a stone, round, still and solid. Just standing beside him felt good, easier somehow. *Am I coming down with something? I mean he's cute as hell. And an artist, which is cool. But what else? He's —*

"What?" Cole asked, and Hank realized he had been staring. He shook himself.

"Let's get you into a wetsuit."

"Oh." Cole's face fell, closed up in nerves.

"Won't take long," Hank said. "I picked out a couple yesterday."

"Okay..." Cole followed Hank into the breezeway of the dive shop, hugging his arms at the change in temperature from the sunny outdoors.

The stockroom was laid out to catch the wind, so things would dry easily. The Red Sea's steady evaporation, and the height of the mountains at their back meant Al'Shahin was sweltering and muggy, despite its proximity to the Sahara. The same evaporation was why the water was so clear, so Hank didn't mind.

"This is where we will come every morning and get our gear. I have the gray truck this week. Borrowed a smaller boat — it's tied up in the next cove. I already loaded the tanks and things for later." Hank went through his usual spiel, safety brief and equipment lay-out, but he watched Cole, noting his attention wavering. He was agreeing with Hank's suggestions without really hearing them.

"Hey," he barked. Cole startled and turned those big brown eyes to Hank. "You gotta pay attention, sir."

"Please call me Cole," he said. "I'm sorry. I'm nervous all of a sudden."

"I'm going to take good care of you," Hank said. He realized how that sounded and cursed internally. "I mean, you have nothing to worry about. It's just you and me, and you are going to love the places we go. We gotta get through this part, though. So pay attention."

"Okay, Hank. I will," Cole said. He put on a brave smile and focused on their gear.

Hank swallowed. *He says your name, and you fold like laundry. What the fuck is wrong with you? Go to Sharm this weekend and cruise the Dancing Crab, get your dick sucked so you can be professional.*

That was bullshit. Hank had stopped visiting Sharm el Sheik's tiny gay scene as soon as he got into debt to Khaled. There was no time. Every chance to dive was money in the bank. And anyway, as Sam had pointed out, giving Khaled more leverage was a terrible risk. Hank shook his shoulders out.

Leverage included making moo-moo eyes at the fucking guests.

Chapter Five

Cole

Grande Diving had no changing room. Which meant peeling off his shirt and wriggling the shortie wetsuit over his trunks, sweating and cursing and wrestling the neoprene on—all under Hank's watchful gaze. He helped a little, gave advice, but generally left Cole to it. Which Cole appreciated, except he couldn't see Hank's eyes behind his shades and his face looked—

"What are you so pissed about?" Cole snapped, yanking off the second too-small suit. Only a last-minute grab spared him from flashing his crushed junk as the wetsuit dragged his trunks off.

"Hey," Hank said, crossing his arms. "It ain't my fault the wetsuits don't fit."

"What the—?" Cole finally managed to yank up the next wetsuit, adjusting his junk. The fellas were shoved up between his miserable sweaty thighs. His back itched, he was sweating like a whore in church, and this fucking guy—

"This damn shop," Hank continued. "They cater to so many teenagers—I can barely get regular people fitted anymore. Another thing that makes me crazy here. I'm always borrowing suits from other places."

Despite not being able to see Hank's eyes behind his shades, Cole sensed Hank was being truthful. Why did he scowl so much then?

"Hell, you didn't think I was making a dig at you?" Hank said. He pulled the glasses off, rubbing the bridge of his nose. "I'm sorry, sir. I would never—"

"Stop fucking calling me sir!"

The shades went back on, the scowl settling again, like a door slamming shut. Cole regretted his outburst. How to *walk it back*, as they said at work? The *sir* thing was clearly an extension of Hank's badass act, along with his scowl and stupid sunglasses. Cole turned his back, reminding himself that he didn't care at all whatever this guy thought.

A few tugs here and there, and Hank gave a nod of approval.

"All right. That's the one. I'll make a note of it and it will be yours all week."

"Two weeks."

"Oh yeah?" Hank asked, his scowl replaced by an honest-to-goodness smile.

"Look at that. You do know how to smile!" Cole laughed. He couldn't help it. Hank had a *dimple*.

"Very funny. Let's get you a BCE." The smile vanished, but at least it wasn't replaced with the scowl again. "BCE stands for—"

"I already did all my testing," Cole said. He jabbed his fingers along the wall, pointing at each piece. "Buoyancy compensator, weight belt, regulator, back up regulator, pressure gauge, dive computer —" He rattled them off.

Hank's expression went from surprised to pleased to grumpy again, some kind of eyebrow calisthenics that never quite reached the rest of his face.

I can't follow this guy's moods. What is going on in his head? Is he okay?

"I'm here two weeks," Cole said, coaxing the smile back onto Hank's face. "And I have so much leave I will probably be back soon enough after that too." He laid an unthinking hand on Hank's wrist, caught up in the big diver's smile. Oops. Cole snapped it back as if burned, fussing with the neck of his suit.

"You can push the top of your wetsuit off, now we know it fits," Hank said, putting his grump face back on. "Let's get to the water."

* * * *

When Cole had been a little boy, he'd dreamed of flying. Despite being chubby, near-sighted and uncoordinated, Cole had plenty of friends. For one thing, his older brother Tobey started shaving in middle school and was taller than even the teachers. No one bothered Cole as long as Tobey was around. And for another, Cole was unfailingly friendly and fun. He couldn't score baskets, but he painted the dragon mural on the gym wall. He couldn't kick a ball, but he ran the fundraiser for the soccer team that let them get to the state finals. He was on every committee and in every club, welcome wherever he went.

Despite this, when he started having the flying dreams, he kept them to himself. He became obsessed with the idea, painting tiny crawling cars on ribbon-thin roads, filling sketchbooks with grids of cities seen from above, and all around the blue, blue sky.

After a short skills check and safety briefing, Hank loaded them onto the boat and took them around the headland to a quiet cove. Quiet as in no other boats or divers, but also quiet on the boat. Hank kept his scowl as they geared up and got into the water. Since Cole was wrestling with nerves, he didn't mind as much as he normally would have, and jumped in as soon as he was clear.

He shivered as the water worked its way into and under the wetsuit, cooling his itchy skin and slowing his rattling heart. He settled his respirator, shifted a little, and signaled his 'okay' to Hank.

Hank gave the signal back, and Cole released the air in his BCE, trying not to flail as he sank down, down, down under the water. It was nothing like his pool dives. Anxiety made him fuss with his mask, equalize until his ears squealed, fuss with his mouthpiece, weight belt, equalize again, and again, fuss with the neck of his BCE vest...

Hank took his elbow, steadying him and indicating they had arrived. Slow and smooth, Hank tipped forward until he was horizontal, still holding Cole's elbow. Doing the same only required mirroring Hank's calm, now smiling eyes. Level, he made sure he was neutrally buoyant then gave Hank another 'okay'. The only sound was his breathing, an inverted cascade of bubbles.

Then he turned, and his childhood flooded over him again.

They were flying. A current moved them along at a leisurely drift, requiring no more than the occasional flick of a fin to keep up. At thirty feet down, the water shone bright and clear around them. Below was a city, the coral tenements packed with fish of all kinds and colors. Tracks of sand ran between like roads, with passing lines of fish like crisscrossing commuters.

Hank and Cole soared slowly overhead, surrounded by blue, as shafts of sunlight shone and shimmered between skyscrapers of coral and stones. It was so exactly like his dream. Cole blurred the past and present in his mind. He breathed steadily — easy to do when it was so loud in his ears — but he recognized he was near tears. Not wanting to get snot in his mask, he swallowed and let his body go slack, the current doing all the work. They drifted at a steady clip, the landscape unspooling below them like drone footage, like — Cole couldn't think of anything to compare it to.

It's so beautiful. It's so beautiful. The colors. Look at that! And there! Purple coral! Gold! And the fish! I'm flying! We're flying!

He wanted to grab Hank and hug him. A gift — it was a gift to experience this. This wondrous soaring glide over the corals. Squeezing Hank's arm would have to convey his feelings for now. Hank's eyes found his and whatever he saw there made them crinkle happily. Nodding, Hank pulled Cole sideways, a brisk kick enough to pop them out of the current.

Now they could get closer, moving along the sandy 'roads' and look at the fish in their condos. Hank swam ahead in a slow side to side, arms crossed, keeping his fin movements as small as possible. Cole imitated him as best he could, continuously distracted by the world around him.

The coral at street level were gray, only some flashes of color on the edges. Fish zipped in and out, busy, cleaning their homes, hurrying from one place to another, defending their little apartments. Cole was no more interesting to them than a passing cloud. They were too busy to do more than glance at him. If lines of laundry had appeared between the coral stacks, they would not have been out of place. When he cruised overhead, the fish all flashed indoors.

I'm a passing cloud. Get inside before it rains. Giggling, he checked his air. Nine hundred still. Good. *Look at that! That silver there, against the blue – how would I do that?*

Nebula of tiny orange fish swirled around a huge purple fan, their tails all flicking the same way as the currents shifted. He rolled to his back, staring up at the edges of the canyon above them, the fish traffic zigzagging across in neat lines. *Air traffic control is busy. And that green. Maybe a heavy oil paint in blocks.* Entranced, Cole bumped into Hank's feet.

Hank untangled them patiently, still moving with the slow, careful grace of earlier, keeping them over bare sand while he steadied them. Cole grabbed Hank's arm, tilting sideways again. His excitement bubbled in every direction. Why had he put this off for so many years? He fumbled for Hank's hand, squeezing it in both of his.

Thank you, thank you, thank you I have never seen anything so beautiful I'm so happy I want to paint it all I want to –

Bubbles erupted around Hank's mouthpiece as he laughed. He nodded, running a hand over Cole's head, taking a momentary grip of his hair. They revolved slowly, Cole trying to project his joy without words, tangling their gear, kicking the sand. Hank agreeing *yes, yes I understand yes. I love it too. Nothing is better than this. Yes, Yes.*

Suddenly, Hank's eyes widened and he gripped Cole's arm, turning him forcefully around. His hold was absolute, and Cole went instinctively still, shivering in amazement.

A huge shark, fifteen feet if she were an inch, cruised the open water above them. A magnificent thresher, her scythe tail waving lazily, she curved in their direction through the beams of sunlight, her silhouette clear in the blue.

When she passed overhead Cole held his breath, every primal instinct in his body shrinking back, even as his intellect thrilled. His heart a wild tattoo in his ribs, he gasped, releasing a cloud of bubbles. She made a leisurely arc, close enough to touch, and soared off beyond the reef edge. They watched until she was only a flash of silver in the deep blue.

Chapter Six

Cole

Cole had no shame about crying. It was simply a thing he did when happiness overwhelmed him. And clambering across the deck of their boat, balancing on Hank's strong arm to the bench, Cole was dizzy with joy. So he cried, laughed, cried some more and waved off Hank's worried smile, blinded by sunlight and white sky.

After everything was put away, wetsuits pushed around their waists, faces toweled, sunglasses on, they sat side by side, Cole vibrating with joy. Hank had his usual scowl, his gaze inward, drinking water. His bouncing knee eventually shook Cole out of his comfort. He stood and made his way carefully through the gear to the back of the boat, letting the sun heat his clammy skin. He was still shivering, but it was a deep personal thrill.

It feels like a first kiss. Everything is different. The blue swells around him gave no indication of the wonders below. A secret world. Yes, it was exactly like the first kiss. Like losing his virginity, a private ecstasy — there was no outward sign of how profoundly the world had changed. But it had. God, it had. He wanted to howl, to shout his joy to the red cliffs. Hearing the clink of the tanks, the patter of Hank's feet coming closer, he spun around.

"When can we go again?" he asked, turning a little too quickly. Hank caught his wrist, his eyes hidden behind shades.

"Get out of the sun, sir. You are going to burn."

"Sir?" Once Cole had steadied himself, he slapped Hank's hand away. "Aye, aye, Captain!" He gave a smart salute and nearly tipped again. Hank caught him by the shoulder this time, and for a brief glorious moment, Cole was pushed up against that rock-hard body, hand flat on Hank's left pec. Which, incidentally, was swimmer-hard, and at eye level. Hank didn't have much in the way of chest hair, but what he did was scattered with gray and curled down like landing lights into his wetsuit.

Cole did not put his face on Hank's chest, for which he deserved a medal at least. Instead, his wetsuit tightened miserably as desire swept over him. The smell of Hank's skin was compromising his safety mechanisms, letting in a litany of invading thoughts. Foremost was the idea that he was completely alone at sea with a man who checked all his boxes.

"This way," Hank muttered, guiding him back under the awning. The cool scratch of his palm on Cole's back sent goosebumps flashing up and down his arms. "I told you, we have twenty minutes. Then another dive, then lunch. Take advantage and fill out your log."

Cole's joy slid away. Of course. Hank did this every single day. The opening of a whole new world for Cole was just a Monday for Hank. There was nothing special about what they had done. Well, that certainly helped with his wetsuit problem. Glaring at the wide back curled away from the rest of the boat, Cole stuck his tongue out at him. Petty but satisfying. Another memory surfaced. A book he had purchased for his nephew. Cole stifled a bark of laughter.

"What?" Hank said.

"You ever seen a grouper?"

"Course. You wanna see one? There's one lives by a rockfall about two clicks from here. I call her Gladys."

Cole shook his head. "Don't change your plans. You remind me of a kid's book, called *Grumpy Grouper*."

"Very funny. I ain't grumpy," Hank said, turning his back again. "I just got a lot on my mind. Real big serious things. So big. So serious."

He gave a loud harrumph, and a moment of excruciating silence pressed in on them before Cole burst out laughing. He dropped onto the bench, catching the twitch at the corner of Hank's mouth. Okay, so the grumpy grouper bit *was* an act. Cole was mostly sure now. Mostly.

The real grouper didn't show itself until the very end of their second dive, even though they looked all over for her. But when she did, the big fish's face was the one in the children's book. Gladys was nothing like the monster groupers Cole had seen snorkeling in Florida, but she was a couple of feet long, and looked exactly like Hank. Cole conveyed this through a series of hand gestures while Hank pretended to ignore him, arms crossed, body floating idly in the current.

* * * *

As ordered, Cole had packed himself a lunch from the hotel's enormous buffet. A plate of greens, tomatoes and some nuts for protein. He wasn't on a diet, no matter what the lady in the spa thought. But if there was one hold-out between Cole and his self-esteem, it was strangers watching him eat. That, according to his therapist, made sense since Donnie had been such a dick about it. But despite all the work he had done, and all the joy he had rediscovered in eating with friends, he drew the line at eating in front of Hank, magic dive or not.

His stomach grumbled loudly, but he told it to shut up — Rome wasn't built in a day.

"Is that what you brought?"

"Yes," Cole said, fingers tightening on his takeout box. "I like a light lunch."

"That's not enough," Hank said, his scowl returning. "A salad isn't enough."

"What?" Cole understood Hank's words, but the meaning eluded him. *Not enough of what?*

Hank leaned over, holding out a spoon of his rice. "You need a lot more calories. Here, try some of this," he said.

Cole wasn't sure what possessed him but, instead of taking the handle, he took the offered bite. When he closed his mouth around the silverware, his eyes shot to Hank's, saw the raised brow. An awkward second drew out, with Cole hyperaware of his tongue pressed against the warm, round underside of the spoon.

He pulled back slowly, pretending to focus on the food and not on what else Hank could put in his mouth. Well, that was one for the group chat. He could almost hear them. Laura would immediately declare Hank a top and want to know every detail. Elia would be applauding Hank's take on the whole thing. She was Cole's source for all things body-positive.

"This is good," he said. And it was. His tastebuds roared to life, saliva flooding his mouth. He closed his eyes to appreciate the delicious rice with egg and were those olives? And spices and nuts... His worry about being watched receded even as he tried to guess ingredients.

"Here," Hank said. "I brought plenty." He shoveled more onto Cole's plate—half covering his salad. "I like to cook."

"Thank you," Cole said. "I try to eat right and—"

"Why?"

"Because I want to be healthy."

"You're definitely healthy," Hank said with a snort. "You swam for an hour straight, twice, and you ain't even breathing hard."

"Well, if I am going to be swimming a lot, I want to look good in a bathing suit."

"You do."

"What do you mean?" Cole's mouth went dry. Had Hank just—did he? Had that been what it sounded like? Hank looked away, coughing.

"Sorry," he muttered. "That was inappropriate."

"Did you just compliment me?" Cole's heart gave a little stutter.

Hank's ears darkened, and he stared firmly at his rice, jabbing at it. "Yeah," Hank said finally. He shot a glance up at Cole then looked back at his rice. "I'm sorry. I should mind my business."

"I liked it," Cole said hastily. "Really. God. Uh, that's nice." *Nice? Really? Laura is going to laugh me into next week.*

"It's true," Hank continued, still murdering his rice. "I mean, if it's okay to say. You, uh, you look good. Real good. You don't need to change. Your body, I mean. Jesus Christ!" He slapped his rice onto the bench and buried his face into his hands.

"I am so sorry," he groaned from between his fingers. "I'm going to get myself fired." This was light-years from what Cole imagined from Hank. The divemaster was…was he *shy*? Was that possible? If the grumpy thing was because he was shy, and not because he wanted to be some badass, then Cole Hadley was in trouble.

"Do you always hit on your students?" Cole teased, despite the completely out-of-control butterflies in his belly. He had another mouthful of rice — were those currants? "I bet they all fall in love."

"Never!" Hank blurted, straightening up. He pulled off his shades, searching Cole's face. When he saw Cole believed him, he subsided, leaning against the bench and dropping his head back, wrists loose on his lap.

Cole's toes curled in his dive boots. Was this really happening?

"I usually have the opposite problem," Hank said. "The divers think I'm an asshole."

"Why?"

"Because I am," he said, head still back. Cole tried to ignore the long line of Hank's throat. The muscles bunched on his shoulders, muscles Cole couldn't quite remember the name of. *What are those called? Those big shoulder muscles. Trapezoids? Whatever. He is trying to flirt. And it's awful. Bless his heart.*

"Not that I have noticed," Cole said. Honesty and kindness warred in his heart. "I mean, maybe a little?"

"It's just that when people are careless, it's dangerous. And not only dangerous to them — all them crosses at the Blue Hole ain't for show — it's dangerous to the reef. They flail around, try to touch things, kick the coral... It makes me crazy. This is one of the last really pristine reefs in the world. Asia is full of trash. The southern hemisphere ones are bleaching like crazy. The Caribbean is overcrowded. There just aren't many places like this left."

"I like hearing how much you care," Cole said. So he'd been wrong about Hank then. Wrong on every front, except the hot Daddy vibe. That hadn't changed. But Cole was wrong about everything else. Hank was passionate about his work. It made the diplomatic wheels spin in Cole's mind.

He knew someone at Nat Geo. Could he connect Hank? Should he? This man he'd just met might have zero interest in Cole's help. Really, it was time to turn the work brain off. "But what about the serious divers? There have to be people like you."

"There are," Hank said, glum again. "But they don't stay at the Grande. They dive in small shops. And those are closing down. Besides..." Hank shot another one of those shy little smiles. "They don't know the places I know. Special spots, like where we went today."

"So it's not a coincidence that we were alone?"

"No," Hank said. He squinted up at Cole. "Is that creepy? I don't want to weird you out."

"Not at all," Cole said, gathering his courage in both hands. Another mouthful of the delicious rice helped. Time to shoot his shot. "Alone at sea with such a hot guy? How could I complain?"

Hank stiffened, ears darkening again.

"You're messing with me," he said in a low voice, going back to his rice murder. "'Cause I made that comment about your body."

"Not messing with you, but yes it's because you said that…and because it's true. You're *very* hot."

A soft silence stretched this time, gentle, the very sunlight around Cole seeming to hold its breath. Hank fussed with their gear, shades firmly on, but with flashes of smile he tried to hide. Cole took some more photos of the cliffs, and a few more of Hank, who was *definitely* smiling now. The butterflies were back, bigger and…flappier? Cole basked in the feeling, let it pour through him.

It was fun to watch Hank fight the smile sneaking through the corners of his mouth, to see the lines on his forehead smooth out. Of all the things Cole had supposed about Hank, a thin veneer of toughness over a marshmallow interior had not occurred to him any more than humidity in the Sahara. But here he was, sweating over both.

After the requisite surface interval, they got back into their gear, still in the same breathless silence, slipping under the surface with barely a splash.

Chapter Seven

Hank

Hank was having a terrible day. Or rather, he was having an incredible, perfect day — which was terrible.

For starters, it had been months since he had seen a shark so large. That was a profound, visceral thrill. But as incredible as it was — she'd come so close! — it was the least interesting thing that happened. The other things were, in no particular order, Cole's tears. Cole's laughter. Cole's wide hand on Hank's bare chest. The bulge in Cole's bathing suit. The way Cole ate now that Hank had made it clear he needed to. *When he closes his eyes and goes 'mmmmm' at my cooking should not be that level of porn, but it is. Why?* He was already planning the menu for tomorrow — which would include dessert.

But most of all it was the dives. Cole was natural in the water. He didn't flail or thrash around or kick his legs in every direction, the way everyone did when they dove for the first time. He was so contained, bobbing along, staring at everything. He didn't suck down all his air in ten minutes. They had been able to get all the way around the bell tower reef and still had two hundred psi left in the tanks when they paused at their safety stop.

Hank could tell by Cole's clench on his hand that Cole got it. Cole felt what Hank felt when he dove. Most people loved it. But the number of people that understood, were bitten by the real bug, becoming lifelong divers after one dive? One in a million. And Cole was that one. *He called me hot. Said it right out.*

His tears had made perfect sense to Hank. A dive as ideal as that one, for a first time? It deserved joyful tears. Except Hank was fighting a cloud bank of depression. He made himself look at Cole as little as possible…he failed repeatedly. *He called me hot.* Hank touched the spot where Cole's hand had rested, right over his heart.

You can't. You know you can't. You've already said too much. Is it creepy? Am I being a creep? No. He's a grown-ass man. It's not creepy, it's desperate. It's sad and stupid. Think of that hot Jordanian guy from last month instead. You didn't thirst over him this hard. And his dick was so big it slipped out of his —

"Hank? Did I lose you there?" Cole waved his logbook. He had filled in the details from their first two dives. The depth, times, the conditions, how much weight he carried — all the rest.

"Sorry, I was…" *Thinking about cock. Like a goddamn loser.* "What's your question?"

"This whole section here, what do I put?"

"You put anything that happened which you want to remember. They will all start to blur after a while. And it's nice to have a record."

"Okay." Cole bent over his dive book and began writing in a neat angular hand. Hank tucked his hands into his armpits. It was that or touch the little pale strip of skin at Cole's hairline — his tender neck with its damp curls. Hank turned his back.

"Don't forget the shark."

"I won't forget the shark as long as I live," Cole said quietly. "Anyway, I drew her portrait."

He flipped back a page and held up the log. Sure enough, curled around his descriptions of the reef and lists of fish was a beautiful abstract thresher shark, seen from below.

"You did that?" Hank said. "Lemme see. Damn, you really are an artist."

"Thanks!" Cole said. His little bear ears and the cheeks above his beard went pink.

"And just with a hotel ballpoint..." Hank continued. The shark was lovely, the twist in her body, the lean power of her muscles indicated by no more than a few hash marks and shadow. It conveyed the moment exactly.

"But how did you do this light beam?"

"Oh, I just left that empty, like negative space?"

"Would you...?" Hank cleared his throat, fighting the urge to touch the nearest ear. "Would you mind drawing one for me?"

"Sure! Where's your log?"

"Oh, I got so many dives now, I don't even log them no more. I'll give you some paper back at the shop."

"I have a sketch book," Cole said. "I didn't bring it because I didn't think I'd need it. I've carried a sketchbook with me everywhere since I was twelve. But..." Cole's round nose scrunched. Hank had never seen someone so cute in his life. "Well, I told you I was in a bit of a slump? This—" He held up the shark, his eyes shining. "This is the first thing I've really done in a long time."

"It's amazing," Hank said, wishing he was more articulate. "You're really talented." Cole's expression was somewhere between self-deprecation and wonder. His thick fingers traced over the shark.

"Bring your sketchbook tomorrow," Hank said, ideas falling over one another in his mind. What places would inspire Cole? *Where can I take him? The Blue Hole. I'll take him to see the free divers. Show him the beam cliff.* "I've got a plastic tub we can use, make sure it stays dry."

"Thanks," Cole said, straightening his shoulders. "I will. Just in case."

* * * *

Before going in to meet Sam, Hank took a detour to the side of the shop to change. He moved slowly, his limbs heavy *A hot guy. Very hot.* The words, the scene played itself over and over. He'd complimented Cole without thought. The idea of Cole self-conscious? Terrible. But then—

"He's confident, actually." A quick glance showed Hank no one had heard him. He shook the shirt out, deciding if *confident* was the right word. Maybe. His mind swung back to Cole's hands, tracing the shark. Strong, workman hands, with square fingers.

Hank adjusted his collar, got his keys and wallet, all while thinking about Cole. *What I wouldn't give to have those hands on me. Maybe he said I was hot, but what would he want with an old salt like me? I'm ten years older than him. He's so smart though, and creative and—*

Hank forced his thoughts away. It was time to pay Sam, then he could go home and plan dives to coax more art out of Cole. And food. He needed to get to market before it closed. He —

"Come in, Hank," Sam called, hand over the mouthpiece of his mobile, as Hank neared the office.

His chair squealed in protest as he leaned back, continuing his conversation. Whoever was on the phone, Sam wasn't happy. He was speaking too quickly for Hank's Arabic, but something was wrong. Sam glanced at him, an angry glower making him sit up straight. Shit. Had someone seen…what exactly? Nothing. No. It couldn't be that. What then? Another furious look and sweat trickled down Hank's back.

"I'll tell him! It won't happen again."

Two phrases Hank did understand. Oh hell. *Please please, God, don't let this be Khaled. I can't go work for him. I can't. Jesus. Help. I need help here.* But help was not possible. It never had been. Friends, family — no one he could turn to for this. Maybe Cole — Shame shriveled Hank's belly. No, not Cole.

Sam tossed his phone onto his desk and rolled his head on his neck. Still facing away from Hank, he said, "Why, Hank? Why do you complicate my life?"

"Sam —"

"My life is simple, a delicate balance!" Sam said. "And you. You upset that balance! Now I have my fucking mistress threatening me because you made my *wife* that almond cake."

Hank didn't take in much after that. He answered mechanically, fighting back hysterical, *grateful,* laughter. Yes, he had forgotten that he needed to bake two. Yes, he knew how important it was for a man in Samir's position to maintain peace. Yes sorry. Sorry yes. *Jesus fucking Christ.* The relief was melting his bones, sagging him in his seat.

"I'll make her one," Hank said, thinking of the raw almonds coming into season. Maybe one for Cole too? "And I'll do the little rosewater cake she likes too."

"Good." Samir reached under his desk, pulling out the leather money carrier he kept for Hank's payments. "Now I assume you are here about this?"

"Yep," Hank said faintly, straightening up. He handed Sam his tally, watched as his boss tucked it, along with a thick wad of cash, into the pouch. "I'm ahead a month this time."

"Stay that way," Samir said with a smile. "If I lose you, I lose half my business!"

"Thanks, Sam," Hank said. Relief was still rolling goosebumps up and down his back. "I appreciate it."

"Now get out of here and get some sleep. And stop ruining my domestic peace!"

* * * *

Hank drove back to his apartment with the windows open, reliving the roller coaster of a day. How such pure...bliss...gave way to terror and came back again so fast.

"He said I'm hot. I think he meant it. I think so." It wasn't as blissful to think about. In fact, it was making his stomach roil. "It ain't fair. Why does he have to appear now?"

The shadows of the mountains had no answer, so he drove home after the market, torn between longing and worry.

As Hank mixed batter and roasted almonds in his oven, he wondered if Cole had really meant what he'd said. It had just been so damn long since he'd dated. He needed more recent information. Would Hank feel better if he asked someone? But who? None of his friends, besides Leila and Samir, knew why he was stuck in this backwater town. Any of his dive buddies, of which he had many, would immediately offer to help. But that Hank couldn't accept.

No one else has to pay for my stupid shit. Besides. All those guys want to talk about is how much pussy they score and how many meters they do.

There was one exception. Hank's face lit up as he thought of it. He could call Levi! Levi who never judged, and always had good advice. The fact that he was a hero, a cave diver with dozens of rescues, never seemed to go to his head. And most of all, Levi was gay as a parade and had even worse luck in relationships than Hank. At least Hank's ex had left his bank account alone.

"You've reached the voicemail of Levi Cunningham. This mailbox is full," a robotic voice announced when the call went through.

"Oh, for cryin' out loud!" Hank tossed his phone onto the table. Of course. Perpetually broke Levi didn't have a functioning phone. Who else? Maybe Leila. When was their next card game?

Until then, Hank had better focus on business, not this high school BS. Keeping Samir happy. Booking students. Paying his debt. Not teddy bears. Business.

Chapter Eight

Cole

A dawn hush covered the dive shop when Cole arrived the next morning. He looked all over for Hank. He checked the equipment room, the office—no one. When he reached the truck, he found Hank asleep in the back, head cradled on an inflated BCE. He was snoring quietly, and Cole took a moment to admire Hank's body looking lax and soft. One of his big hands lay face up, and Cole was sorely tempted to touch that cupped palm, the thin tender skin of Hank's inner wrist.

Instead he pulled the release cord for the BCE, deflating it all at once and dumping Hank into the bed of the truck with a *clunk*. "Wakey wakey, grumpy grouper!"

"Damn it! What?" Hank popped up, rubbing his eyes. "Oh, it's you. Good morning, sir."

"This sir thing again?"

"It's more professional," Hank said with a dignified nod. "Reminds me to mind my manners."

"Well, I hate it." Cole laughed. "It makes me feel old, and anyway it's too early for kinky stuff."

Hank's expression at this made Cole's heart sink. Tragically, the earth failed to swallow him, and a tsunami did not come and wash him away. Instead the sun blasted cheerfully, peeking above the horizon, illuminating Hank's astonishment, and Cole's frozen horror with perfect clarity. Nature — terrible friend.

"I mean..." Cole cleared his throat. "You know what? Let's just, strike that from the record, shall we?"

Hank didn't answer, clambering out of the truck bed and rearranging their gear. Cole failed at all his good intentions as Hank bent over to move the tanks. His thighs were strong, the cords behind his knees clear as he moved. And his ass, well, Cole was not a robot. Hank's ass was small, tight, with deep dimples on either side of his narrow waist. He looked away just as Hank turned.

"Consider it struck..." he said with a grin. "Hey, I brought you something."

"Oh yeah?"

"Look on the front seat."

"Wow! What is that?"

"It's a camera — for underwater."

"I know it's a camera! Are you kidding me? You're gonna let me use this?"

"Yep. I hardly use it anymore. And you're the artist."

"Why are you being so nice to me?" Enough was enough.

"I just thought you could take some shots of things you want to sketch later. Take the pressure off maybe?"

Rubbing the back of his head, he rushed the rest. "And I'm nice because you seem like a good person, and you get it. The dives I mean."

Cole stumbled, his heart running like a dog off its leash. *Take the pressure off. Does he mean* — "What pressure?" *Please don't make me like you more than I do, grumpy grouper. This is very unfair.*

"Well, you said you can't pressure your art block?" Hank said. His hands stayed deep in his pockets.

That means he heard what I said. Thought about it, and came back with a gift. A gift that isn't trying to fix anything. Cole's therapist would be proud of him for even recognizing what had happened. If Hank was on a charm campaign, then it was working. Cole's systems were reaching critical.

The camera was a good one, if a little old, with a wide lens and side handles. It had a light on a flexible arm. Cole regretted dumping Hank into the truck — a little. "This is a good camera!"

"It takes really good stills," Hank said, shuffling his feet on the concrete. He managed to maintain his scowl, but Cole could tell he was pleased. "I took pictures of all the little nudibranchs one year."

"Nudist what?"

"Ain't you a cut-up this morning? Nudibranchs are these tiny little slugs — bout like this —" Hank held his fingers a couple of inches apart. "Crazy colors."

Cole was sorely tempted to hug him, but the divemaster was back in grumpy grouper mode, eyes behind shades and hands deep in his pockets. Cole let it go. The promised plastic container for his sketchbook was there, as were three others, packed with food. Lots of food. Hank had cooked for him? *He did. And is that cake? He made all of this? For me?*

Cole took a moment to look at the hills above the resort, moved in a way he couldn't quite identify. Against the pure innocent blue, they were crisp silhouettes, brown and gold in the dawn light. With the white stucco of the little bungalows in front, their terracotta tiles matching the earthy tones — the view could have been from any time in the last thousand years. *Oils. I'm really thinking oil paint. Like thick. Let's see what this dive has in store. But it feels...right. Something is right here.* The joy filled him like clear water. Filled him to overflowing. Filled his well.

"You ready?" Hank asked.

Cole shook off his reverie and hurried to the passenger side of the truck. "Absolutely. I can't wait!"

* * * *

"First dive today ain't one of my secret places," Hank shouted over the roar of the engine and rush of passing air. The truck had a bench seat which was sixty percent cracks and tears. There was no radio, no AC and the windows were manual. Cole loved it. There was something about the glorious dawn light, bouncing along the rutted track, the heat increasing minute by minute, their dust-trail fanning behind them. It felt like adventure.

"Where are we going?" Cole asked.

"Blue Hole!"

"Wait. I thought beginners couldn't dive the Hole?" If it weren't a serious topic, then the jokes would tell themselves. But this was a serious topic, so Cole missed them, which was a crying shame.

"You're with me!" Hank said, face split in a wide grin. He peered over his sunglasses. "You ain't scared of a little hole, are you?"

"Yes!" Cole shouted, smacking Hank's arm. "People die in that hole!"

"No hole ever killed me." Hank peered over his glasses again, and Cole finally caught up. Heat flushed from crown to toes, and he buried his face in his hands.

"Oh my God, you are making ass jokes?" The conversation replayed in his mind in a horrific loop. Hank's grin was addictive. It felt like a secret revealed. Cole reveled in it.

"We really are going there, though. There are things I want you to see." Hank slowed, craning sideways to look for cars before bump bumping them onto the main coast road. Now they could speak without yelling. "We won't be diving the whole thing, just a really nice wall, like a slope really. Then we'll skirt a little section of the hole, watch the free divers for our safety stop. I think you'll like that."

"Are you sure it's safe?"

"Don't worry, sweetheart," Hank said. "I'll take care of you."

Another phrase to hang in the air between them. Hank's knuckles went white on the wheel, and he snapped his eyes forward. Cole looked away, let his hand ride the currents of hot air out the window, replaying Hank's words over and over, sensing in fascinated horror how that phrase rolled through his body, waking the butterflies, tightening the skin on his neck, pushing into his chest, compressing his heart which beat harder in defense.

That was a low blow, universe. Not fair. That was a really low blow. Hit me right where it counts. Right in the feels. Now I have to survive the day just to tell Elia and Laura. Not fair. Not fucking fair.

Walking across a pool deck in full SCUBA gear was hard enough, but the walk from the truck to the entry point of the Blue Hole was a nightmare. They hurried to beat the growing crowd of divers, their booties providing minimal to no protection from stones, jagged or smooth or slimy with garbage. Wearing every bit of gear, including the weight belt cutting into his hip bones, the equipment and tank on his back weighed fifty pounds. Cole would have died rather than show the slightest weakness. His therapist shook her head in his inner eye, asking him what the hell he had to prove.

He kept his outer gaze on Hank's back, trying not to slip or stumble, and ignored all the divers left and right, most freshly arrived and putting on wetsuits. Many of the local guides greeted Hank, smiles everywhere they passed. Hank, head down, kept greetings to brusque nods. Every language of the levant, plus German, some Russians — complaining of course — flowed around him. The stink of sweat and burned fish and diesel fuel assaulted Cole's labored breathing. The only benefit of sweltering, bent like a mule, was that the wetsuit contained his sweat and his thighs didn't chafe. His balls, however? Another story.

Trudging up the hill, they passed the memorial wall. Hank gave it an absent pat, but Cole stopped in his tracks, horrified. Names, plaques, crosses and dates covered the stone by the passage to the ingress. All the people who'd died on *this* dive, in *this* place. *But I have Hank. And he is going to take care of me.*

Swallowing back his nerves, he hustled after Hank, staying close to him, drawing comfort from his calm.

"Okay, time to get in the water," Hank said, stopping at last. Cole looked around. It was just rocks, rocks as far as the eye could see, in the water and out.

"You sure?"

"Sit here. Put on your mask and respirator. Then I want you to scoot forward, turn and drop through that crack right there. Only when you drop to the ledge — fifteen feet down — then put on your fins."

Cole stared at him, his brain not responding. "You are shitting me right now."

Hank lowered them gingerly onto a rock, their legs dangling over the edge into the water which lapped up over their knees whenever a wave came through. The proximity and heat of him settled Cole again but did nothing for his racing heart. The water sloshing around his legs cooled him off, tempting him with refreshing little pulls. Again the urge to prove himself, to impress Hank, snuck in. He pushed it away.

"Take a slow breath," Hank said softly. "I am going to be right here with you. But only one person can go through at a time. Do it in slow, careful stages. You'll see me the whole time. I'm not taking you anywhere dangerous — I'm having too nice of a time with you."

Cole searched Hank's eyes. The glare of the sun made it hard to see, but he believed him. He trusted him. But he was also crushing hard, wanting Hank to like him. And the sense in his heart of wanting to impress Hank was suspicious by itself. *Don't get too far ahead. His eyes are just pretty. What matters is he is a great divemaster, and his focus is totally on me. That's all.*

"Okay, Hank," he said and did as instructed. The bare rock channel was a tight fit, but not claustrophobic. It immediately opened to the sea, as soon as he was under the ledge. Spotting the next ledge below, he let himself sink, slowly releasing the air from of his BCE.

Almost as soon as he landed, he saw Hank's feet turn and drop. Cool water flooded under his wetsuit, making him shiver—no other possible reason at all. They helped each other into their fins, and Hank took Cole's elbow, guiding him into the blue.

* * * *

Driving back, Cole dozed in the passenger seat, the sun warming his clammy skin. After the water, the heat was welcome, soporific, taking nothing from the dream-like atmosphere.

He'd wrapped himself in a couple of dry towels after peeling out of the wetsuit with a sigh of relief. After Blue Hole, and its astonishing free divers rising and falling on their lines like beads on a string, they'd visited another shore dive site, eating Hank's food in the shade of a stone wall. When not complimenting the food, Cole had talked about the color blue in its infinite variations. Hank had beamed, clearly proud of himself.

"*I was hoping you'd like that. The free divers scare my pants off but it's beautiful to watch.*"

"*The way the blue doesn't just darkens, it changes shade...*" Cole had seen thick blue paint on a heavy brush, up and down, like the freedivers, rising and falling. He'd wondered how far out they could go, catch more shades?

Gratitude buoyed him every time he glanced at Hank. Especially since he caught Hank looking at him nearly as often. It was getting harder to pretend something wasn't happening. And Cole wasn't sure he wanted to pretend. *He is a good man, caring. And God, he can cook. I'm gonna nap for days.*

"I wanna show you something," Hank said, waking Cole from his doze.

"Yeah?"

"It's nothing big, but we're gonna go right past so…" Hank drummed his fingers on the steering wheel.

"Sure, why not?"

They rode in silence, warm and comfortable. The extra dark sunglasses were welcome, as was the bottled water Hank pressed on him.

"Okay. Here we are."

"Where?"

They pulled onto the side of the road, onto a flat, dusty space, a few pieces of trash tucked against the rocks. Hank parked and got out, waving Cole with him. A truck roared by, kicking up dust and fumes.

"What am I looking at?" Cole asked. It looked like a place teenagers came to make out. From a wide level lot, a pile of bulldozed rocks dropped to a narrow stony beach. The dark blue water indicated a deep well between the shore and the reef beyond. Behind them was a cut in the hills, letting the sun blast down on them. Cole was glad for his hat. Hank began to explain, arms gesturing.

"So you park here, and the shop is there, a pier past the rocks, a boat can be here on the inside, then the pier would go to the reef. Building in an L shape, so there can be classroom and storage too."

"A dive shop?"

Hank stuffed his hands into his pockets. Cole was coming to recognize the gesture. Hank containing himself, assuming an outward indifference.

"You are going to open a dive shop?"

"One day," Hank said. "I got a ways to go yet. But I own this little patch. From the rocks there to about where that bottle is."

"Wow!" Surveying the scene with new eyes, Cole saw it all clearly. "Yeah, I can see that. You'll get the wind. The rocks could be moved, made into a patio." Hank was pleased, Cole could tell. The big divemaster started picking up rubbish, adding it to the net bag he kept for ocean trash.

"This place is my secret," he said. "I bought it when I first got here."

"How? You're American."

"My friend Leila bought it with my money then gave me a thousand-year lease. I tried to sell it once…" He hid behind his scowl again. "Anyway. She wouldn't let me."

"When will you start building?" Cole asked.

Hank's shoulders bunched around his ears and he shrugged. "Someday."

"I'll paint a mural on your walls!"

This made Hank break out into a smile—the sun coming from behind the clouds.

"I'd like that. It would mean a lot to me. I'll pay you in more lessons."

Cole held out his hand. "Done!"

"Done."

Hank was quiet the rest of the way, chewing his knuckle, his face completely closed off. If Cole had to guess, the big diver regretted showing Cole his piece of land. Why? Cole wasn't sure, but there was something brittle there. Cole sensed a fine spiderweb of cracks under Hank's surface. *I know what that's like. I feel that way about my sketchbook. I wish I could tell him I'm not going to mess with him. That I respect him, no matter what happens.*

Was anything happening, though? Cole was beginning to think that, yes. The flirting, the touching, the shared joy of their dives, even the care Hank took— feeding him, making sure he drank water and took breaks. Something was there. Something…

Chapter Nine

Hank

The next morning Hank had a beginners' class again. Which turned out to be a welcome distraction. The same group of Tel Aviv kids, ready to take their tests in the shallow seas beyond the house reef. They knelt in a circle in the sand, surrounded by curious fish and reviewed hand signals, practiced clearing their masks, demonstrating the various skills Hank had drilled them on all week.

Instead of the usual boredom-driven frustration, Hank felt calm, relaxed. He let them take the tests twice, brought them to the surface to talk before trying again. His patience paid off, and he signed their log books, stamping their certificates to send to PADI when they got home.

Clean-up was a relaxed, happier affair than the last time. Even the little firecracker blonde kissed both his cheeks when he took her wetsuit to hang up. Now that he bothered to find out, he knew her name was Mariam and that she was pursuing medicine. *Something you almost missed out on.*

"Thank you, Hank," Mariam said. "I can't wait to tell my friends! Now we can dive in Greece next year!"

"You're welcome," Hank said, his cheeks heating up. "I think—"

"Oh God, there's that fat guy again." Mariam's boyfriend gave the kind of laugh that would have put Hank's fist through his face in any other circumstance. *But Cole's right. He's just young and stupid.*

Cole was dashing up their way from the beach, his arms full of his bag, smile visible all the way from the shop.

Hank followed Cole's triumphant run, shading his eyes with one hand, the other on his hip. If it weren't for the kids leaving class, he would have laughed and waved. Cole's face a beaming sun, rising pink and shining. *Improves my day just by seeing him. Damn. Let me not get soft in front of these kids!*

No such luck. Cole ran straight into his arms, picked him up and carried him for a stumbling step, nearly sending them over the lip of the terrace. When Hank saw the sketches, he understood. Pages and pages of shapes and scenes. Fish and seagulls, long-legged women sunbathing on the pier. Clouds and random doodles—and Hank.

Seeing himself in Cole's bold style sent Hank's heart into overdrive, so loud he could hear it. *Me? That's me? He drew me.* There was a little cartoon grouper next to his own face in one corner.

"I want one of these! You have to draw me one," he insisted. "I'll hang it on my wall. Me and my namesake."

"You can have this one," Cole said. "You can put it as your picture on the website!"

Their laughter met shock and disbelief from the students, who were taking extra-long to put away their stuff to gawk at them.

"Is that his boyfriend?" Mariam said in Hebrew. "So cute. I die."

Hank's shoulders stiffened. So did Cole's. *He works in antiquities. Of course he speaks Hebrew.*

"This is great, Cole." Hank busied himself with his own gear, piled on the golf cart—they were taking the boat today. "Get your stuff and let's get out of here."

"I brought it down earlier," Cole said. "Didn't want to waste a minute."

"Wait until you see what I made for snacks," Hank said. *God, his smile would power a city.* The work Hank had done the night before was instantly worth it, roasting and seasoning four different kinds of almonds, getting up early to buy fresh dates, packing three kinds of olives. A whole melon, from Nader's rooftop garden, was the treat. Hank was strict about mixing alcohol and boats. *I learned that lesson the hard way, didn't I?* But he had a bottle of white wine in the cooler for their return.

"You brought cheese?" came the cry from the front of the cart. "Oh my God, look at these nuts! Where did you get this bread?"

"I baked it," Hank said, ignoring Mariam's approving nod.

Cole's head popped around the side of the cart, mouth open. "Are you real?" Cole laughed. "We have a whole spread, and the camera, this is going to be the best afternoon! Okay, I have to taste these." And he popped back around again. Mariam's elaborate thumbs-up made Hank shove his glasses over his eyes.

I didn't know making someone happy could have such a low cost and high pay-out.

Cole was exclaiming over each kind of nut, talking about complementary colors of the olives or something. Hank only cared about the brown eyes, and the shy, "Thank you so much, Hank. This is beautiful," that he got when they were ready to go.

There it goes again. My name on his lips. I'd about kill someone to hear that. And if he says it while licking olive oil off his finger like that, I may have to off my own damn self.

"Let's go," was all he said, though.

* * * *

"You see things different," Hank said, rubbing a towel over his dripping head. "Let me see that fan again?"

Cole pointed out the patterns of blue and green in the photo. He had framed a huge fan coral against the surface, focusing on a single orange fish.

"I'd never have thought of any of that."

"But do you see what I mean?" Cole asked, hesitantly. "I'm not being some know-it-all asshole, am I?"

"Hell no!" Hank leaned over Cole's shoulder to point at the screen. "See that there? That blue means another coral is forming there. The color is clear because of how you focused. I mean I really would never have noticed."

"Thanks," Cole said with a grin.

He scrolled through some more shots he had taken, pointing out glimmers in the waves — things that Hank knew intimately but had somehow missed. *It's like I ain't been paying attention. Like I needed this to remind me to open my stupid eyes.*

"Cole?" Hank didn't even know how to express what he felt. Cole's *delight.* There was no other word for it. His delight at everything — the intensity with which he listened to Hank's lessons — the way he saw the world? It made Hank dizzy, tearing away at his apathy, upsetting the indifferent shell he had built around him. His distress must have shown on his face since Cole stood, putting warm hands on Hank's shoulders.

"Are you okay?" he asked.

"I ain't," Hank managed. "Not at all." He had to know. He had to know. Even if he never acted on it. Even if all he ever got was this change in point of view...

"What's wrong?"

"Did you mean it? When you said I was — uh when you said you liked — listen. This is really dumb but I just gotta know — when you made that compliment..."

"Of course I meant it." Cole laughed. "You kidding?"

"No, I ain't." Hank tried to get his accent under control. It tended to get thicker when he was nervous or angry. "I mean, I'm not kidding."

Cole leaned in, his face mere inches away, brown eyes swimming in and out of focus as Hank's gaze darted from his lips to his eyes and back again. Cole's breath was a warm invitation against his lips.

"I meant it," Cole said softly. His confidence was absolute, even if Hank still wavered. *Fuck Samir and Khaled and fuck anyone else. If I don't do this, I'll regret it my whole life.* He closed the distance and pressed his lips against Cole's. Just a soft, simple kiss. Then he pulled back to look in Cole's eyes, check in.

"Do that again," Cole said dreamily. "I've been thinking about it nonstop for four days. Do it again."

So Hank did it again. This time he kept his mouth against Cole's, tasting the melon from their lunch.

Lapping upper and lower lips, he used only the tip of his tongue. He hesitated, uncertain. But Cole's mouth was so warm, and sweet tasting. He couldn't get enough, burrowing in, licking the corners of his smile. When Cole's tongue slid over his, he shuddered, pushed harder.

The boat caught a swell on the side and rocked them. Their heads bonked, and they staggered a few steps. When Hank went back in, desperate for more, he overshot and ended up with a mouthful of chin. Another swell, and their teeth clicked, sharp and uncomfortable. Hank pulled back again and pressed his forehead against Cole's.

"This ain't going exactly like I imagined..." he muttered, embarrassment roiling through him.

"Here," Cole said. "Let me." And oh thank God he did. He held Hank's face, kept him still and kissed him, exploring and gentle. The unruly flapping wings in Hank's belly subsided, and he sighed into Cole's mouth. The kiss deepened. Hank sucked Cole's plush lower lip, touched the tip of his tongue to his teeth. Cole's blunt fingers scratching in Hank's beard made him shiver.

"Can I touch you?" Hank asked. "I don't wanna overstep—"

"God yes," Cole said. And finally, finally Hank had Cole in his arms. Two perfect armfuls. Hank squeezed him and ran hands over his back and shoulders, up his bare arms and down again, dragging his thumbs in Cole's armpits and cupping his pecs.

"Your body is so great," Hank said. "God, I could just squeeze the life outta you."

"No, you're the one with the great body." Cole laughed, patting Hank's chest.

Hank cupped Cole's chin, holding his gaze. "It's just a work body. Maybe that's why I like cubs like you." Hank ran a gentle palm over Cole's belly. "Wish I had more hair too. I love hairy bellies."

"I aim to please." Cole laughed uneasily, leaning back to look in Hank's face.

"I mean it. I'm —"

The sound of a motor interrupted them, made them part like startled fish — but it was just a fishing boat, paying them no mind. Still. Any reminder of the thousand consequences of becoming involved was enough to cool Hank down.

Cole busied himself with the camera, back turned, his ears red. Hank squeezed the steering wheel, wishing for Cole's body. But it was time to head in. The sun was nearly touching the horizon. He pushed the dive boat back in the direction of the resort. *And it's rummy night. Thank God. Maybe Leila can slap some sense into me.*

* * * *

"Hank, why are you not listening to my scintillating conversation?"

"Apologies. Leila." Hank forced his attention back to his cards. "I was…thinking."

"Who is it?" Leila peered at him with shrewd black eyes.

Hank laid out a card, slowly, thinking of Cole.

"A woman or a man?"

He glanced around, instinctively. Ridiculous. First of all, it didn't matter, not in this city of artists and poets. And second because of course there was no one. Leila was a Coptic Christian, a jeweler, with a beautiful terraced home overlooking the mountains. The moon was down, and they sat in a comfortable glowing circle of lamplight, playing cards and smoking pot, as they did every Wednesday.

"A man then, to make you so jumpy."

"I have met a person," Hank began slowly, choosing his words. This would stretch the limits of his Arabic. And he wanted to be precise. Leila had no tolerance for bad metaphors. "He is good, and happy. He delights in small things, but also big…"

Leila leaned forward, lit a little clove and marijuana cigarette, her cards abandoned.

"He is American. He is my student. He makes me laugh."

"Oh, Hank, this sounds serious. Can it be this man has cracked through your barnacle-encrusted heart?

"You joke. It has only been six days. I have drawn out the dives — took him to far away sites — just to be near to him."

Leila looked positively delighted. "I must meet him! This is the news of the season! Someone has charmed the old shark at last." She fell back in her seat, clapping her hands and laughing.

It was contagious. Hank buried his face in his hands, switching to English. "I don't even know what to think. He's younger than me. He's smart. Works for the government — to do with art at the Embassy in Cairo or something. And I'm just some old salt — "

"Is he interested?"

The skin on Hank's neck squeezed hot and tight, even as Leila's smile bloomed in response.

"You blush? *You?* Oh, Hank — he *is* interested then?"

"I kissed him," Hank said, face firmly in his hands. "And he kissed me back."

He groaned as Leila hooted with laughter. She shouted for her grandson to bring them wine. When it arrived, she poured each of them a glass, settling in like the start of a meeting.

"You have been alone for too long. I was beginning to worry for you. Tell me everything."

With Leila's white hair in a bun, her peering over her glasses, Hank felt called to the blackboard. "It was awkward, but then so good," he conceded. "Made me nervous actually. It's been a real long time." He sipped his wine, gathering his thoughts.

"Oh, my poor Hank," Leila said, patting his knee. "Well, I hope he takes pity on you. Puts you out of your misery!" She gave another howling laugh, drumming her heels on the floor while Hank buried his head in his arms. "Oh, my darling. Habibi, forgive me. I promise once I have this out of my system, I will be a much better friend." Her giggles died down even as she sipped her drink and wiped her eyes.

"You're a very good friend," Hank protested. "Even if it seems like right now you're getting a whole lot of jokey jokey at my expense!"

"Okay. Okay. When will I see him? What does he even look like? Is he also a useless wall of muscle?"

"Boy, you're on a tear tonight," Hank grumbled. "No, he isn't. He looks like a little brown bear, to be honest. I just want to squeeze him until his eyes pop out. Brown hair, beard, looks like a professor…which — I guess he is? He buys art, for galleries and stuff."

"Oh my. This is very serious," Leila said. "This is not some bimbo then. He is a real man."

Something did a slow, joyful roll in Hank's belly.

"Yeah," he said, "He is. He's a real man."

Chapter Ten

Cole

Cole drank his coffee on the terrace of his villa the next day, waiting for the sun to rise. Like the word villa, *terrace* was an optimistic term for a postage stamp of stone with an arch of bougainvillea, enough room for exactly one chair and a small table. Cole thought it was the nicest seat he had ever had.

Before him was the slope to the sea, with its white sailboats sprinkled on the deep blue. In the furthest distance, he could just see the mountains of the other coast. Saudi Arabia shimmered on the horizon, caught in the rising sun as a line of gold. A cargo ship, deceptively tiny in the haze, made its plodding pace left to right, probably coming from the Israeli port city of Eliat.

Enjoying the view and the coffee, breathing the clean air, watching the waving palms and blue-shirted gardeners tending the bristling lawns, were delaying tactics. Cole couldn't even pretend otherwise to himself. He'd spent the night updating the group chat, drawing pages of cliffs and fish and abstracts, all while admonishing himself about Hank.

A mistake. A terrible mistake. You will get yourself sent home. It's February in DC right now. Home meant sleet, ice, Metro packed with tired government workers, all dripping and bundled and sniffling colds. It meant humming fluorescent lights in the State Department back hallways. *Fuck that noise. No dick is worth that. And for him? To lose his job? Hell no.*

But the kiss. The shy, awkward, terrible, *amazing* kiss. The interruption had thrown cold water on the flames. But Cole sensed a furnace inside Hank. A dampened down, smoldering pyre that needed no more than a single breath of air to erupt. And that was dangerous. Cole had masturbated three times in the last twelve hours thinking about it. *Unfair.*

Unable to delay any longer, Cole got up, gathered his bag, and went to the shop. Perfectly divided between caution and lust, he decided there was nothing to do but see what happened. *I'll regret it my whole life if I don't see where this goes.*

* * * *

"So uh, I gotta ask you," Hank began. They had barely spoken a word the whole morning, but now, with the little boat taking them away from the shore, the tension spilled over. Hank wouldn't quite meet Cole's eye, his mouth in its usual grim line. "Yesterday? That was…an accident, right?"

Cole couldn't get a sense of what Hank was asking. *Does he want me to say yes? No?*

"Not…really?" he said. That seemed like a fair compromise.

"I'd like to do it again," Hank said. His hands were jammed tight in his pockets, his shoulders up around his ears. The shadow of the boat's roof cover reflected in his shades. Their boat rocked gently, Hank keeping perfect balance, gaze firmly on the deck.

"Look at me," Cole said, exasperated.

Hank looked up, puffing out his cheeks and rubbing the back of his neck.

"Take your shades off."

Hank did, and Cole's heart began to stutter, a snare drum rattling behind his ribs. Hank's eyes were dark with lust. He was looking at Cole, his body, with uncomplicated, expansive, genuine greed.

"Now you can kiss me," Cole said, and Hank was on him, clumsy, arms clutching and fingers tangling in Cole's hair. He kissed his lips, his cheeks, rubbed his face against Cole's, bumping him into the bench. Cole wasn't much better, doing what he had been desperate to, running his hands over Hank's hard chest and shoulders, down the plane of his belly, shoving at the wetsuit to trail fingers over Hank's shaking navel.

"God, Cole, your body, your body — can I say? God, I love this." He kneaded Cole's shoulders, scratching blunt fingers through his chest hair, making him shiver.

"You do?"

"God yes," Hank said, breathless and grinning. "When you first showed up, I thought you looked like a little bear cub. I was so hot for you. Right away."

"Wait, wait."

Hank stopped immediately, leaning back to look in Cole's face. His lips were red, smile loopy and gentle. It took ten years off his face.

"What is it? Too fast? I'm sorry. I —"

"No, no. Get me out of this wetsuit before it breaks my dick off."

Hank wasted no time, pulling the last few inches of Cole's zipper and helping him peel the suit all the way off. He held Cole's elbow when Cole bent to push it off his waist and had a perfect glorious view when Cole's trunks peeled off right along with the wetsuit. Nothing short of an act of god would have stopped him from grabbing a handful.

"Hey hey!" Cole laughed. "That's not fair. You too!"

They wrestled, pushing and pulling their wetsuits, imitating the wet *shlorp* the suits made. They hung them from the hardtop of their little boat, letting them drip over the side. Their trunks they simply kicked under a side bench with their folded gear, too eager for more. Cole nearly killed the mood by bursting out laughing.

"What?" Hank looked down at himself. "Okay, the tan lines are a little ridiculous. Guess I need to get out more. Or less? I dunno. Don't laugh at me!"

"I'm sorry," Cole said. He trailed bold fingers up Hank's thigh, pausing at the line where the brown skin turned pale. Hank had strong thighs, and they flexed under Cole's touch. "I think it's cute."

Naked at last, they pressed their cold wet bodies together, kissing slow and luxurious in the shade of the cover. Tilted up this way, Cole's mouth was a cup, something Hank could dip into, and he did, drinking and tasting him. Cole didn't resist, offered himself up, dizzy at the thought of it.

Hank pushed back first, looking down between them. He groaned. "God look at you," he breathed.

Cole shivered. He kept his hands on Hank's hips, fighting the urge to hide himself. Hank was hard, uncut, his prick curved with a pronounced head. If Cole had any doubts about how Hank saw him, that bobbing cock, a clear drop of pre-cum already starting to dangle, was proof of his attraction.

Hank closed his hands, gentle, reverent, around Cole's cock. "Jesus, kid," he breathed. "How do you find pants that fit?"

Cole snorted, ducking in for another kiss. He could kiss Hank all day, loving the feel of his beard and soft lips. Hank was noisy, making rough little grunts and groans, lapping at the sweat on Cole's throat.

There wasn't much room between the benches and tanks. Hank maneuvered Cole backward, sure-footed and careful to the long bench. Cole sat, and Hank slid down with him, kneeling between Cole's spread thighs. He looked up, the question clear on his face.

"Yeah," Cole said, curling a hand behind Hank's head. "Suck me."

Hank's eyes were all mischief now, annoyingly aware of the power he had, catching Cole's flustered agreement for what it was — desperation. Cole could count on one hand the times Donnie had done this for him. *No, we are not thinking about that asshole now. Everyone else loves it. His hang-ups were not my fault.*

Hank's tongue, curling and sneaking around edges, made Cole's feet scrabble against the deck. He hissed as Hank's calloused hand, scratchy and strong, jerked his shaft in the loosest possible grip. Cole didn't thrust, but it took all his will power.

He kept his eyes open, taking in Hank's big tan shoulders, with their faded tattoos, and the sweat shining on his scalp. His free hand worked between his legs, stroking himself and mesmerizing Cole as the muscles on Hank's back flexed and relaxed, flexed and relaxed.

"This is so hot," Cole whispered. "God, look at you…"

Hank's eyes crinkled and he pushed down, sucking in tight wet pulls. When he came up again, a thin line of saliva connected his lower lip to Cole's head.

"You are too," he said. "You smack me on the head if I do anything you don't like, okay?"

"No fucking," Cole blurted.

Hank laughed, shaking his head. "Hell no," he said. "Think I have condoms on this rig? I ain't been laid in a year, baby."

Cole relaxed all the way, lolling his head over the back of the bench.

"Besides," Hank continued, sliding his tongue down and around Cole's balls in a way that made him whimper. "I like it both ways, and I like to take my time. This ain't the place."

Cole folded forward, grabbing Hank by the ears, dragging him up into a kiss. Their arms squeezed tight, their mutual excitement conveyed without words.

"Me too," was all Cole could say, in between kisses. "Me too."

"Come on, come on," Hank gasped. "Let's…at the same time."

"Yeah, be on top," Cole said, but returned to his exploration of Hank's mouth. He tasted like garlic and salt, and Cole couldn't get enough. Their kisses were clumsy as they discovered each other, switching from awkward bumps and breathless laughs to slow, careful presses.

Cole held Hank by both cheeks to slow him down, to kiss him carefully, sweetly. It wasn't just that Hank was shy. His very nature was making Cole assert himself, giving space for him to fill. Hank's generosity, that was the right word, raised Cole's confidence, even as it sent jolts of want to his groin.

How can he be like this? He looks like that, and he doesn't have a man? Doesn't have hot twinks hanging on his every word? Sincerity. Another good word. Hank wasn't playing games. Cole, highly attuned to bullshit as he was, felt none of it here. And that made him reckless, made him kiss Hank without inhibition.

Taking the cue, Hank wrapped his arms around Cole, stroking his back. They pressed their bellies together, their thighs, making every part touch that could, their wet cocks rolling across each other, sending little shocks up Cole's spine.

"I ain't gonna last," Hank murmured. "But I don't care. I wanna be good to you. I want…"

They eased down to the deck, Hank tucking a life vest under Cole's head. Some shifting and one barked shin and they were head to toe. Cole's view was full of Hank above him, his long cock bright red and shining. Hank smelled like the ocean, and Cole tugged his hips down, wanting to breathe in close, lick the creases of Hank's thighs and groin, taste every part of him.

Hank licked him again, his breath hot and gusty against Cole's wet balls, making them tighten up. He shivered, swallowing the head of Hank's cock, maneuvering it in his fist. He thought of the spoonful of rice, and the warm curve that reminded him of this, exactly this.

"You taste good," he said.

Hank made a rumble Cole felt rather than heard, vibrating up from between his legs. They were moving slowly now. Cole's balls ached he wanted to come so badly, but the pleasure was too much.

Cole grabbed Hank's ass, digging his fingers in to hold on, head tilted, mouth open in a long groan. He rolled his tongue against the underside of Hank's shaft, rocking his head side to side, making the big divemaster shudder. The power was dizzying. Hank was falling apart, shaking to pieces just from this?

Cole used his grip to shift Hank's hips front to back, controlling the depth of his salty slick cock, but encouraging Hank to fuck into his mouth. Eyes open, Cole took in the shudders of skin, goosebumps and shaking thighs. He watched, his heart hammering as Hank's balls drew up, pairing with the rapid bellows of his belly against Cole's chest. *I'm wrecking him. I'm wrecking him.*

"Cole…" Hank gasped. "Baby, I'm gonna come. I can't hold back no more." He buried his face in Cole's groin, cursing and moaning, his body stiff and shaking. Cole clamped his lips tight and sucked, bobbing his head up. Hank came in long spurts, moaning and grinding his mouth on Cole's shaft.

Hank swallowed him in turn, jerking his shaft with his fist, wet and messy, and Cole let go, thrusting up and rolling his head on his neck in pleasure. He didn't hold back, emptying himself into Hank's mouth, knees wide and heavy. It went on and on, white hot bursts, singing up his spine until he dropped flat, sighing deeply into Hank's thigh. They eased up on each other, gentle licks and soft kisses, finally turning and shifting so they were face to face.

Hank was red and sweating, his grin a lazy, wet-lipped thing, eyes soft as the dawn sky. It was good to be in his arms, their pounding hearts pressed together.

They kissed, tasting each other, tasting themselves, sighing into each other's mouths.

"This might be the worst place to nap," Hank said softly. Cole agreed with a hum, curling his face into Hank's neck. "I'd lie with you all day anyhow. But it's almost time for a special show."

They got up groaning, the fiberglass floor an agony on their shoulders and, anyway, Cole was eager to see Hank's special show. They helped each other into their wetsuits, swapped out tanks and double-checked their gear without words. Neither had anything to say. Instead, they spoke with their hands. Hank held Cole's waist as he stood. Cole stroked Hank's bald head, feeling the faint stubble there while Hank sighed and pushed into his palm like a cat. They touched where they couldn't speak, Cole too full of feeling, a rising sun of joy.

Chapter Eleven

Hank

They would be just in time. After reviewing their signals, they tipped backward into the blue, orienting themselves and easing down, down, face to face and smiling around their mouthpieces. When they reached their depth, they leveled out and Hank took Cole's hand.

They swam, lazy kicks, drifting along the curves of the reef, their tangled fingers as natural as the curious fish that investigated them. Just in time, Hank had led them to an unfrequented wall. There were no other divers, and the pristine reef sat in a ray of sun from a cut in the cliffs above. Like the beam of a flashlight, in the crystalline water the column of light had crisp, defined edges, gold against dark blue, holding up the roof of the sea. Cole turned, eyes huge, to Hank, who gestured with one hand — *ta-da*!

Cole paused, hovering easily as he observed it. He held still, standing upright in the water — a museum visitor in front of a painting. The glow in Hank's heart matched the world around him, the corals turned up to their beam, the deep blue on every side.

The beam was transitory, just at this time of day. Just for Cole. *I've been waiting forever to show someone this. To have a person who'd appreciate it.*

When Hank gave Cole's shoulder a little tug, Cole floundered briefly, coming out of his daze before kicking himself forward to explore.

* * * *

Back on the boat, they were in no rush. They spent their surface interval kissing, lazy and relaxed. Cole clambered onto Hank's lap, straddling him and cupping his beard in his hands. Hank followed Cole's lead but felt awkward, unsure of himself. It was a relief to trust his partner. Cole was gentle and sweet, which did more to soothe Hank's fears than any empty words.

Cole's hands, square and strong, with soft hair on the tops, pushed his shoulders into relaxing, tugged his arms to encourage him, cupped his face to guide.

"I ain't so good of a kisser, huh?" Hank said morosely.

"You're improving fast," Cole laughed. "And we don't even know each other."

"Yeah." Hank hung his head, fidgeting with the bungee holding the tanks. "Aside from the fact that I ain't been with anyone in a while…" He gave Cole a rueful, embarrassed smile. "But kissing hasn't been on the menu in even longer."

"Been a while for me too," Cole agreed.

"Yeah?"

"After my ex there was a guy or two — just hook-ups, I tried Grindr but I was scared to run into one of his friends, so I decided to give it up. Work on myself."

"How long?" Hank leaned his head back to see Cole's face, taking in the way his brown eyes caught the light. He could touch Cole's neck now, and his ears, stroking both with his thumbs in little circles. The troubled look on Cole's face made something hot and fierce roar up in him.

"Two years. But since I've been here, it's more about diplomacy, you know?"

"What do you mean?"

"Egypt," Cole said, rolling his eyes. "The men fuck each other sideways here, but it's still illegal. They give us this briefing—and the Pride Alliance at the Department of State has all these warnings—anyway."

"Yeah. I can hook up here, but I gotta be…quiet."

"Not much quieter than a surface interval on a boat."

"Usually it's about five or ten people, so not really. There was this one guy, kept flashing me his junk. I don't know what he was thinking."

"I do." Cole laughed.

"Almost got me fired."

"Ouch." Cole considered it. "You know I will be discreet?"

"Appreciate it, since I would lose everything if my boss found out."

"This is a bad idea, isn't it?"

"It's terrible," Hank agreed. "A terrible idea. The worst idea I've had in a long time."

"We can stop."

"Only if you want to," Hank said. "I'm not sure I could walk away after today."

"That good, eh?"

"Funny man. I meant—the dives, the things we shared…and yeah—that good." Hank lunged at Cole and wrapped him in his arms, play biting at his neck.

They wrestled a little, grinding and growling. Cole's weight felt so good, soft, squeezable but grounding, holding Hank in place. It was hard not to imagine Cole lying on top of him.

"Wanna practice kissing some more?" Hank said. "I want to see if I can reach level three, get my advanced kissing cert."

Cole hummed, gave a rueful shake of his head. "I only know how to teach Cole-style kissing. It won't help you when you try it on anyone else."

"I don't want any other kind," Hank said. His voice went rough, scratching his throat, and Cole pulled back.

"You mean that?"

"I'm sorry. I guess that was too intense," Hank said.

"Do you mean it?" Cole repeated, giving Hank a little shake.

"God yeah," Hank said. "Even if we never see each other again after this—I got no regrets." *Worth it. Worth it to remember what it's like. How it is to have a man look at me like that. To remember it ain't too late. There's more life out there. More in me. More than I thought.*

They came back with the setting sun, parting ways with barely a nod, under Samir's watchful gaze.

* * * *

Cole

Waiting for his room service dinner, Cole lounged on his porch, watching the distant light of ships on the horizon, sipping white wine and daydreaming about Hank. The buzz of his phone interrupted his thoughts, a damn shame since he and Hank had been on a sailing boat in the Med.

J Calamy

He winced at the stream of missed texts. *Oops.* He should have known his friends would want an update. Propping his elbows on the arms of the chair, he was eager to give one.

Cole: Sorry! I haven't been online all day!
Laura: Why? What exactly are you up to, Coco?
Elia: Why have we not heard from you?
Cole: *shrug* *crossed swords*
Laura: Oh no.
Elia: oh NO
You didn't
I demand details
Laura: Hank the Hunk?
Cole: ... *scubadiver* *eggplant* *eggplant*
Elia: He did. He did it. Oh nooooooo.
Laura: Yesssssssss.

Cole: So first of all, in my defense, I was left totally unsupervised. On a boat, in a beautiful sea, with a giant stack of bricks of a man.

Elia: Everything. Tell us everything. How did this happen?

Cole: So I told you he paid me a compliment, and I paid him a compliment. Anyway we went on this glorious, perfect dive. Then he asked me if I meant it.

Laura: Oh my god, you absolute loser.

Elia: Shhhhhh... I'm with him... I see it. The sea, the sun, Hank the hunk...

Cole: We kissed yesterday. Then couldn't even look at each other.

Laura: Why not?

Cole: He's shy. And we got interrupted.

95

Cole stood and looked down the walk to see if room service was close. No sign of them, so he stretched, breathing in the wind a moment before settling back again. He wasn't sure how to explain it. But the way the kiss had shifted from clumsy to desperate so quickly. When was the last time he'd reacted so strongly to the person he was kissing? Not the kiss, but the person?

Elia: What happened?

Cole: The kiss started really bad. But then it was good, awkward standing in all the gear and all — another boat came by, and so we acted all nonchalant and it killed the mood. He went all aviators on me again.

Laura: What did I miss? Aviators?

Cole: He does this thing where he wears mirrored shades and makes a serious mean-guy face and it's like someone left the chat. I call it grumpy grouper.

Elia: What the hell is a grouper? Never mind. I don't care. I get it.

Laura: So now what?

Cole: So today maybe things escalated a little.

Elia: Escalated how much?

Laura: He says a little

But he lies.

Elia: The lies.

Laura: The LIES.

Cole: So today, we go out even farther and at first, it's all sweet. He's letting me use his underwater camera, and he let me bring my sketchbook and even brought a special container so it would stay dry —

and he has been bringing these amazing lunches every day

also the sun is very bright

and so maybe today we did more
like—a lot more
Laura: You sucked his dick.
Elia: Stop! No. Wait. Cole, quit beating around the bush.
Cole: Listen, I am screaming into my drink here. But yes, we had a mutual session, and the floor of a boat is VERY uncomfortable.
Elia: I am thrilled for you but also very worried.
Laura: I want to know it all.
Cole: Don't be gross. Get your own D to play with.
Elia: What does this mean? Like what happens now?
Laura: It's just vacation D, right? You aren't going to risk anything stupid here.
Elia: He is NOT. The art world is a tiny, incestuous village. Cole. If you get kicked out of Egypt for this—
Cole: Settle down—we aren't stupid.
Laura: …
Elia: …
Cole: You bitches! I swear to God, the lack of support? Tomorrow afternoon is another boat dive, and I am taking a leap, bringing colored pencils. The muse is with me even if you aren't!
Elia: Please be careful. I have to get to work.
Laura: Okay now tell me all the details.
Cole: Ha! The rest stays in my fantasy reel where it belongs.

"Mr. Hadley? Room service here." The waiter appeared, pushing his cart. He placed the tray on the little concrete table with a flourish.

Stashing his phone, Cole tipped him with the same flourish and waited until he was out of sight before digging in. The food was okay. Not even close to Hank's. *Hank. Wonderful, generous, smoking-hot Hank.*

Cole poured himself another glass of wine, settled in watching the distant ships again. Now where had he been? Ah yes. He and Hank were on a sailboat in the Med. Hank had one of those little sailor hats on...

Chapter Twelve

Cole

The next morning, Cole came up from the deepest sleep of his life to the sun already slicing through the blinds. *Shit! I'm late!* He got ready in record time, dashing down the terraces to the dive shop. He hoped Hank hadn't had to wait too long. And that he had a thermos of coffee tucked away.

"Sorry, Hank. I'm ready to go! Oh—" Cole cut off, realizing another man was present. Hank's body language left no doubt that this man was not a friend. And Cole's own inner-warning systems were on high alert when the man stepped forward.

In a pair of nice slacks and a white button-down shirt, he was ridiculously handsome, with swoops of jet movie-star hair, and wide shapely eyes with lashes so long they looked like he was wearing mascara. When he smiled, his perfect teeth flashed in the gloom. Handsome, well-dressed, friendly smile—but Cole's hackles stood straight up.

"Mr. Hadley," Hank said, hands firmly in his pockets. "This is Khaled Said. He owns the Grande."

"Mr. Hadley, are you enjoying your stay?" Khaled's handshake was warm and dry, his forearm flexing where it emerged from his rolled sleeves.

"It's excellent, thank you," Cole said, bringing every scrap of State Department manners to bear. "You must be very proud." He watched Hank out of the corner of his eye. Something was wrong here. Hank was crushed in on himself, holding still and trying to act natural. He looked — fearful.

Cole refused to be intimidated. Cole had not been intimidated since his divorce and he was certainly not going to start for this man, no matter how attractive he was. An entire flock of red flags swooped around Khaled. More than ten years in antiquities automatically meant brushing elbows with unsavory people. Cole didn't even break a sweat.

"I am, thank you. What brings you to Al'Shahin?"

"The diving." Cole matched Khaled's smile, mirroring his body language. Hank Ashton, big as a door, grimaced as Khaled slapped him on the back.

"Has my divemaster been showing you his best spots?"

"Some of them," Cole said, pushing away the flash of anger when Khaled said '*my* divemaster'.

Hank still hadn't moved, the tension around his eyes giving away what his casual pose was trying to hide.

"He's pretty good. I already let some friends at the embassy know they should ask for him when they come. Chief Leroux is an avid diver, and so are a number of the Marines. I'm sure they are looking forward to having a fellow veteran show them around."

Khaled's smile widened. He understood exactly what Cole meant. Hank was a US citizen, and if Khaled did anything to Hank, Chief would have a team of DSS agents here the same day. Fuck around and find out. Hank might be the care-taker in their...whatever this was, but that didn't stop a bear of protective instinct from rearing up in Cole's heart.

A moment of silence, perfect understanding between them, and Khaled gave Hank another counter-shaking back slap.

"It was a pleasure to meet you, Mr. Hadley," he said. His smile, as he started up the path, never got as far as a smirk. Khaled was too savvy for that. But his opinion of being threatened by a little fat guy in flip flops was clear. Cole turned to Hank the moment Khaled was out of sight.

"Who was —?"

"Let's go," Hank said. He wouldn't meet Cole's gaze, hustling them over to the golf cart. While part of Cole wanted to demand to know what was happening, he recognized that he had known Hank a week at this point. And so couldn't be surprised that there were things he didn't know, even if his feelings were galloping away with him. And anyway, golf cart meant boat, and boat meant hours alone. And hours alone meant plenty of time to talk, and other things.

The bitterness of it was killing Hank. He had no idea why Khaled had chosen this moment to make an appearance. Generally, Hank only crossed his path once a year or so. But why now? Was it a coincidence? Hank badly wanted to ask Samir, but worried that asking would be tantamount to admitting he had something to hide. No, that didn't make sense, but he was helpless to stop that particular anxiety.

I ain't exactly sneaky. Everyone says I'm a terrible liar. Why now though? Why right now, the moment I catch a glimpse of something else. Something beyond all of this?

"Hank."

And now Cole was going to ask questions. Hank pushed the bitterness away again. Tried to. Cole would suspect something was wrong. God, the way he had stood up to Khaled. Perfectly contained. The image of a stone returned. Cole as an immovable boulder, smooth and round and impossible to dislodge.

"Hank, are you all right?" Cole's hands on his waist fit Hank's thoughts, holding him still and solid. Soft lips pressed his shoulder, belly against his back.

"Yeah," he managed over his shoulder. "Yeah, I'm fine."

"Did this Khaled guy bring you bad news? You aren't fired, are you?" Cole's voice was as warm as the rest of him, right by Hank's ear.

"No." Hank waved off Cole's worry. "He would send Sam to do that."

"It isn't my business." Cole's voice was as warm as the rest of him, right by Hank's ear. "But if you ever need any help, we, I mean the Embassy —"

"No." Hank waved off Cole's worry, a bitter twist of shame in his gut. "Don't worry about it, sweetheart."

Cole's gaze was far too shrewd for Hank's present state of mind. *If you need help. If you need help.* A mental image of Cole, in a shirt and tie, shaking hands with important people, managing to threaten Khaled without shifting his smile. *Guess I forgot that my sweet little artist is actually a diplomat.* Totally out of Hank's league, Cole Hadley was...someone. Hank couldn't decide whether to laugh or cry. *I am falling so hard for this guy. All I can offer him is these dives. It's all I got to give him.*

"Let's get in the water." He focused on driving the little boat, swinging them out beyond the hotel's home reef and around the next headland. He didn't speak until they set the buoy anchors.

"Okay this next dive is a real simple one. Just a leisurely drift like we did the first day. But if we're lucky, we'll see a cool friend."

"What kind of friend?" Cole asked, letting the previous subject drop.

Gratitude quenched Hank's worry, releasing a sigh like steam. The scene replayed itself in Hank's mind. Cole, cool and aloof, face to face with Khaled, not in the slightest bit intimidated. *And now he ain't holding it over me. He's minding his business, but I know he's got a million questions. God, I wish I had answers for him.*

Once in the water, everything slowed, sparkling with joy of the deep, a sunken fishing boat, an octopus! A black-and-white sea snake undulating through the water. Cole hanging upside down, perfectly comfortable, to photograph the underside of a huge fan. Hank reckoned if his heart beat any harder when Cole smiled, he'd use all his air.

He can't be real. How can he be a soft cuddly bear and still stand like a superhero this morning? What the hell am I going to do?

"What did you make this time?" Their dive finished, Cole pulled out his sketchbook, already settling in his usual spot to capture what he had seen. His strokes were fluid now, the resulting sketches needing less adjusting as he went. Cole's big square hands, delicate and precise over the paper, fascinated Hank. He

Drifting

fumbled into the boxes without looking, his gaze fixed on the octopus emerging under Cole's pencil.

"That crispy fish like the other day with the lemon sauce?" Hank passed dishes and forks over and settled by Cole's side. "I tried to make coconut rice, but it came out kinda sweet. So I made it into rice pudding, real low-country with honey and all? Turned out great."

Once they were settled, Hank helped Cole remember details, made sure he ate and refused to think about Khaled Said even once. The sketchbook and lunch safely out of the way, the kissing got serious. They rubbed their faces together, soft and heavy-limbed. Hank's pulse was a living thing between his legs, greedy for the taste of Cole's sweat.

"It's about time for us to go back," Hank rasped. He was not done. Not by a long stretch and an idea occurred to him. "I want to take you somewhere special."

Cole's laughter set him back a moment, until he was bowled over, wrapped in wet clammy arms and warm soft belly, flat on his back, kissed breathless.

"You need to stop!" Cole shook him by the shoulders. "It's done. I'm impressed! I'm so impressed. You don't have to try anymore."

Breathless with laughter, Hank rolled Cole over and rubbed his face in the soft hair on Cole's chest. "Look. I can't take you to my place. Everyone knows me," he said, nipping the skin over Cole's collarbones.

Cole shivered, running his hands over Hank's back. "And you can't come to my room," he said. "You'd lose your job."

"Exactly. But listen, I want you. Do you want me?"

"Hell yes. I've been jerking myself like a sixteen-year-old since I got here!" Cole laughed, grinding up against Hank's thigh.

104

"Damn. Good. Good. I'm going to pick you up in town. And I'm taking you to the desert tonight—I have some Bedouin friends. They run those night tours, but since I send people their way, they let me use their campsite sometimes."

"To seduce wayward men?" Cole asked, smacking Hank's shoulder.

"No! To be alone. To be quiet. To watch the stars. I take dinner, and I bundle up and stay up all night."

"God, that sounds amazing."

"So come with me tonight. Let me show you some geology, feed you dinner then fuck you sideways all night."

"Easy there, killer. I may be the one fucking you, you know!"

Heat flared in Hank's navel, a shivering excitement. The gleam in Cole's eye sent goosebumps all the way down his legs.

"That would be…okay with me." He held his breath, waiting for the laughter. It didn't come.

"Seriously?"

"I told you. I like everything." *No one ever lets me bottom, but him – do anything for him.*

"Then let's go camping. See what you mean by everything."

"I'll get you at six. From your usual patio."

"My what?"

Hank realized he had given himself away.

"I seen you, sometimes," he said softly, head hanging. "You making friends everywhere. Everyone loves you. I only watched a little. I'm not a creep."

"Why didn't you come over?"

Hank shrugged one shoulder, letting that stand for his entire situation. What else could he say? Cole stroked his head, pressed his lips above his brows, making him sag.

"Yeah, I forgot for a moment there," Cole sighed. He wriggled in closer, laid his face on Hank's chest. "Now I get what my closeted friends meant."

"You never had to hide?"

"Nah, I was lucky. I had a big brother who could bench press a bus. Anyone messed with me and Tobey would have beat them down. I didn't realize how lucky I was until I went to college and saw how hard some had it."

"Lucky is right."

"Were you in the closet?"

"For a time." Hank could laugh about it now. The shower rooms at Basic Training had been a revelation to small-town North Carolina boy Henry Ashton. "But it was more about not being sure what I wanted, not knowing what any of it meant." The recognition in Cole's eyes made him continue. "I joined the Navy for a bit and realized real quick it wasn't right for me, but I also learned about myself there too."

"You'd be so hot in one of those little white hats," Cole said, fanning himself.

"Funny guy," Hank said. "I may still have it somewhere. If you're a good boy. I'll dig it up for you."

"In that case..." Cole sat up, a wicked grin showing he knew damn well his round ass was grinding right over Hank's prick. "I'd better be very good."

Chapter Thirteen

Cole

When Hank had said "desert camp" Cole had pictured a tent like he and his friends took to the Shenandoah, a small lightweight thing, an air mattress and a campfire for s'mores.

This wasn't that.

They left the truck at a parking lot and got on a four-wheeler, riding through the valleys and canyons. Under the eyes of the other tourists in the parking lot, Cole leaned back against their cooler and bags. But as soon as they were out of sight, he wrapped his arms tight around Hank's middle. Holding his man was nice, but also practical. He was so stunned by the beauty of the stone he would have fallen off otherwise.

The campsite appeared around a jumble of fallen orange stone, nestled in a little valley, facing east. Three huge tents, tall enough to stand in, surrounded a large fire pit with a clay oven and picnic table. There were low wooden seats around the campfire, looking horribly uncomfortable until Hank opened one of the tents and began pulling out cushions and blankets. A stainless-steel cart, missing a wheel but propped onto a brick, held pots and pans, plates and cups, knives and anything else.

"We'll sleep in that one," Hank said, jerking his chin. "Go set up the bed. I'll get all this ready."

"Did you say bed?"

"Sure did. Go see!"

A bed. Raw wood like the other furniture, no more than a foot off the ground and covered in a drop cloth to keep off the dust, but there was a real mattress, and clean folded sheets and blankets and rugs under the cover. The floor of the tent was covered in more carpets, and colorful hangings brightened every wall. The smell of woodsmoke and incense, something floral, teased his nose. A Thousand and One Nights promised by every detail. *This isn't Arabia, Cole. But still, they really are pulling the whole Bedouin vibe here. Gorgeous. I wonder who did the textiles?*

Cole couldn't help the thrill in his belly as he made the bed, thinking of what they were going to do. The chance to sleep together? Not only sex, which Cole was pretty damn excited about, thank you very much. But actually sleep together, touch, kiss, eat — all without inhibition? That was almost more exciting. Almost.

Hank built the fire, humming to himself and bending over frequently, to Cole's delight. The firelight, once it was going, made stark shadows. Hank's shirt pulled tight across the wide expanse of his back. The strangeness of Hank in clothes — in a pair of butter-soft old Levi's and a gray Henley with a missing button, exposing a hint of collarbone, was ratcheting up the desire in Cole's belly. He was glad he had thrown a pair of cargo pants in his bags, as well as a sweatshirt.

They watched the sun set from the top of the hill behind their campsite, then wandered down in the afterglow to feed the fire and make some tea. The stars were spilling across the sky, more and more of them, the kind of view Cole had never experienced in his life. It was breathtaking, like being in space. They pointed out planets, constellations. Satellites made their way in eerie straight lines — thrilling to see. Hank checked his watch repeatedly for "a surprise" as if Cole wasn't already bowled over.

"Okay, almost...almost...there!" Hank said triumphantly. Cole saw another satellite, much brighter than the others, still making that uncanny perfect arc. "That is the International Space Station."

"No!" Cole said wonderingly. "Really?"

"Really. I looked it up, and she will zip overhead a couple of times over the next few nights."

"That's amazing," Cole said. The idea moved him, of the astronauts aboard that light crossing the sky. He waved, couldn't help it. To his relief Hank did too. As natural as saying "cow" when one grazed in a roadside field. "How did you know I was a secret space nerd?"

"I didn't." Hank laughed. "But that's great news. I'm a giant space nerd too. Living on a submarine cured me of wanting to be up there though."

"I bet!" Cole still had his Smithsonian key pass. In another world, he would take Hank into the bowels of the Air and Space, finally have someone to talk to about it. *In another world.*

"Nothing else looks like that," Hank continued. "It's moving at seventeen thousand something miles per hour — while we sit here."

"Imagine riding in a star," Cole said, swallowing past the sudden pain in his chest. "*Living* in a star."

Hank cleared his throat and began to recite.

"The stars are mansions built by Nature's hand,
And, haply, there the spirits of the blest
Dwell, clothed in radiance, their immortal vest;
Huge Ocean shows, within his yellow strand,
A habitation marvelously planned,
For life to occupy in love and rest;
All that we see – is dome, or vault, or nest – "

"That's beautiful," Cole said. "Did you write that?"

"Hell no," Hank laughed. "It's Wordsworth. There's more but I forget. And I only know that much cause my mother made me memorize poems when I was little. I had a speech impediment, and she busted heaven and earth to help me." He leaned back on his hands, a soft smile visible in the firelight.

"That is the cutest thing I ever heard," Cole said. "I bet you're a big ol' mama's boy."

"Hell yeah, I am! She lives in Statesville. In her eighties and still helps my sisters with all my nieces and nephews."

"Why are you so far from home, Hank?"

"Well…" Hank rolled a stone back and forth under his foot, clearly choosing his words. "The Navy gave me the travel bug. I did my four years, saw the world, realized I didn't like the Navy part and didn't re-up. I had a big breakup around then."

Cole pressed his lips to Hank's shoulder and kept them there.

"I took some time to wander. Learned to dive in Thailand, came to Egypt twice, and the second time I…just sort of stayed here."

Just sort of stayed. That was one way to put it. *I sank someone's boat. I didn't have the money and was headed to jail so I took a loan from a bad fucking man. And I been trapped here ever since.* Trapped, and now presented with another reality. A reality that could be his. He could simply bail. Why not? Because every penny of his debt would be taken out of Samir, who had vouched for him. Because Khaled was certainly not above squeezing even Leila, and he knew that Hank understood that. So Hank stayed. He couldn't do otherwise.

"What about you?" he asked, covering the stab of pain in his heart. "How did you end up here?"

Cole pushed in a little closer, his breath in pale clouds outside their blanket. They were snug together, though Hank's nose was getting cold. He didn't care. Cole's body held heat like a stone, and Hank wanted to lie on him like a lizard, suck all that heat up.

"I got my MFA," Cole said, "and a friend runs a terrific gallery in Baltimore. I curated her gallery all summer trying to get a job with Smithsonian. I loved it. One day a lady came in, said she curated for the Department of State. All I had to do was apply for the foreign service. Got a job at Smithsonian in the meantime, in antiquities. A basement job. Like the sub-basement. Dust allergies so bad I had to get shots!"

Cole's laughter made Hank pull him tighter. *He is so damn cheerful. Stuck in some sub-basement looking at dusty stuff, and he sounds like it was the funniest thing he ever did. I need some of that mindset.*

"But then I got a divorce. My ex-husband was... He was bad. Really messed with me. So I got really deep in my job and applied for the Foreign Service. It took a couple years since I was a fucking mess, getting a divorce and all. But I passed the exam. The Cairo posting came up, and I jumped at it."

"So your ex," Hank said cautiously. "You got away from him, I guess."

"I was already on the way before I posted here though," Cole said. "I'm lucky. Like really lucky. I have good friends and a good family. They helped me get my shit together. I got into therapy and really worked on myself."

"Damn," Hank said. "I admire you so much."

The words hung in the air, worrying Hank. Was it too much?

"That means a lot," Cole said. "Can I be real here?"

"It's dark. It's just you and me and the stars," Hank said. But his belly coiled with dread. The speech was coming. The *"you're nice but"* speech. The *"I have to go to my fancy job in Cairo and can't take my vacation dick with me"* speech.

"I don't want to leave."

Hank blinked. Reviewed those words in his mind.

"Because of the diving?"

"Yes. And Al'Shahin. The artists, the whole thing. But mostly you."

"Me?"

Cole shifted around. They couldn't see their faces clearly, but Hank could make out Cole's rueful smile.

"You have bulldozed into my head," he said. "When I watched you move that coral, when I saw the way you were so careful? It… It made my head spin."

"That's decompression sickness," Hank quipped, flailing at the emotions swirling up around him.

"Funny man. I mean it. I don't know where this is going. I love my job. I love Cairo, despite the traffic and pollution. My whole life is fantastic. But you make me want to move here."

Hank shivered, cleared his throat, tried to regulate the wild beating of his heart.

"I'm sorry," Cole continued. "Is it too soon to say that?"

"No," Hank rasped, clutching the blanket tighter around them. "Everything is different since you came. Everything is...better."

He didn't say more, caught in the quiet around them. The space between them was like one of the geodes he found in the desert sometimes. Where their hands joined, the secret inner chamber. Wind-shaped, battered on the outside, shining crystals on the inside. Their blanket was another layer, the desert another and the stars another. Concentric rings pushing his awareness inward, closer, to the space between them.

He held that space, breathed into it even as he pulled Cole to his feet, pulled him to the tent.

Chapter Fourteen

Cole

The kiss happened without thought, a natural part of what they were saying to each other. Once inside, they shimmied out of their clothes, still under the heavy blankets, Cole relished the sharp bite of his shorts scraping over his cock. When his calves hit the bed, he stumbled, sucking hard on Hank's lip.

"Wait—"

Hank pulled back, leaving Cole reaching in the dark. Some fumbles and curses and a click then a lantern appeared. Cole blinked, eyes adjusting to the glow from Hank's cupped palms.

The light was small, not reaching the dark in the corners. It was a circle, warm and intimate, which fit the space between them. Suddenly Cole was acutely aware of his thighs, the stretchmarks on his hips, and his arms came up to cover himself.

"I like it better dark," Cole said, the words rushing over each other. "Lets me relax, you know — lets me — "
Lets me hide. But I don't need to hide.

"I want to see you," Hank said, tilting sideways to catch Cole's eyes. "I'll turn it off if you want but — "

Of course, of course. This is Hank. "Okay," Cole said. "You know what? Yeah, I want to see you too."

"I can't wait to be inside you, baby," Hank said. "You've got me shaking." He pressed Cole's hand to his belly, let him feel the tremors there. "Look at me, Cole."

Cole opened his eyes. A tear slipped free, trailing brightly down his temple to his ear.

Hank stopped his movement and leaned forward to press his lips to Cole's cheek. "What's wrong?"

"I'm not used to being looked at like this," Cole said. "I'm good. Happy. It's just...a lot."

"You believe how bad I have it for you, right?"

Breathing hard through his nose, Cole nodded.

"I want you to enjoy your body," Hank said. "I want you to see how much you turn me on."

Another tear slipped free, and Cole nodded again. Hank leaned forward and used his dry hand to stroke Cole's cheek.

"We can stop, you know," Hank said. "There are a lot of other things we can — "

"Hell no," Cole said. He managed a shaky laugh. "God, you really mean it. You really mean all of this."

"Look at my dick, baby." Hank shook his hips, making Cole let out a little snort of laughter. "I'm pushing fifty — I don't get hard like this unless I want to. Unless there is someone who blows me away. And

I've had more stupid hard-ons since I met you than... Damn I don't even know when."

Hank patted his hard belly, not flat by any means, but hard.

"I'm nothing special," he said. "I just spend a lot of time swimming and carrying heavy tanks. Guess I was always kind of a dumb jock you know?"

"Don't call yourself dumb," Cole said. "And you look special to me."

His hands followed his gaze, tracing along Hank's ribs, chasing goosebumps. Hank's nipples pebbled hard under Cole's dragging thumbs. He shuddered when Cole tugged at them. "You look like a mean boss top." Cole stifled a laugh. "I bet the word *Daddy* just falls out of guys' mouths!"

"Hell yeah." Hank caught Cole's laugh. "Ever since I started losing my hair and shaved it." He got the laugh under control and stroked down Cole's face. His rough palms sent jolts across the skin of Cole's back. "And sometimes that's good. I like nailing some soft thing against the wall as much as the next guy. But sometimes...I just want to let go."

"I have the opposite problem." Cole's heart battered around in his ribcage like a bird in an attic. "I'm all soft and jiggly. So men think they can ride right over my feelings. But I'm bossy as hell when I want to be."

"We'll take turns being bossy then." Hank laughed. Just like that. No hang-ups, no posturing.

"Deal."

Their kissing got messy, unfocused mouths alternating between lips and throats. Their tongues pressed and parted, Cole rooting into Hank's belly, nipping the tender skin over his hips.

"Goddamn," Hank breathed. "I hope you're ready for how bad I want you."

"Oh yeah? Think you're going to get this?" Cole laughed, wriggling.

Growling, Hank grabbed two handfuls and kneaded. Cole had stretch marks on his hips, and Hank wanted to lick them, wanted to push his face into every inch of soft skin.

"Hank?" Cole breathed. "Can you top first? I just... I want."

"Of course, baby. Lie back," Hank said, and Cole did, moving slowly. "Is this okay? I want to see your face."

Cole nodded eagerly.

Hank nudged himself forward until his lean hips were tight against Cole's bottom. He could feel the heat of Cole's opening against his shaft. Taking the oil he'd packed, he covered his hands and began to massage Cole's belly, the muscles of his hips, his upper thighs. The smell of musk and roasted spices filled the tent. Cole's nostrils flared, and he whined, low and urgent. Hank's hands were chased by warmth from the spices. Cole's skin drank it in waves.

Hank shushed him thoughtlessly, tracing slick fingers over Cole's stretch marks again. Cole squirmed, but Hank wasn't having it.

"Wanna make you feel so good, baby," Hank said quietly. "Let me take care of you."

Cole relaxed, letting his eyes slip closed. Did that make it easier to hear as Hank began to murmur compliments, praising his lover in a steady tone?

"Beautiful, everything about you. You're gorgeous and soft, but strong. I can't believe I get to do this..." It wasn't the most sophisticated litany but the more he talked, the more Cole squirmed, his cock hardening even though Hank never touched it. Hank complimented Cole's body, his skills in the water, his desirability. Cole's head rolled as Hank worked his hands over his chest, tugging at his nipples.

"I think someone has a praise kink," Hank laughed, teasing Cole's cock with his fingertips.

"I can't help it," Cole gasped. His cheeks were flushed, his smile radiant. "You're making me feel so good."

The oil on his navel slipped down between them, and Hank rocked his hips, sliding his cock between Cole's buttocks — grinding himself against Cole's opening. He could feel it, still furled, a ridged mouth against his shaft.

"You deserve it," he said. "You deserve every good thing I could do for you, baby. I'd take such good care of you. I could..." His words trailed off.

"You're giving me a heart attack," Cole croaked, voice hoarse. "Please touch me..."

Hank's words were coiling under Cole's sternum, bringing him dangerously close to feelings that served no purpose at all. Hank reached for the lube, dragged on a condom.

"Spread your legs, baby, show me what you want," he said.

Cole moved slow, feeling a looping smile wobbling on his face. Pulling his knees up and spreading them, he curled further, offering himself up.

Still murmuring praise, Hank squeezed out some of the lube and rubbed it between his fingers.

He gripped Cole's left leg under the knee and pushed, folding him almost in half. He rested his greased fingers gently against Cole's opening, using only the barest pets, tiny circles—like he wanted to savor the moment. Cole squeezed his eyes shut, and he panted lightly, feeling his face crumple in worry and anticipation.

"You're perfect," Hank rasped. "You got the sweetest little pink hole. I can't wait. I can't wait to be inside you."

Cole said nothing, but he drew in a hitching breath. His opening softened, and both fingers slid into his core, stretching him. It was smooth, frictionless and divine. His mouth fell open, helpless. Hank's callouses petting the delicate tissues, twisting with his wrist— Cole wanted to scream, it felt so good.

"More, Hank. Oh shit, more," Cole said, his voice ragged with the deep flaring need for *more*.

"Yeah, baby, okay. You're opening up so sweet for me." Praise fell from Hank's lips as he added a third finger, stroked in and out. "You are soft as silk. I can feel your muscles working, beautiful, beautiful..."

Cole arched his back and moaned, open-mouthed. *If I do nothing but kiss this man and jerk myself on his fingers it would still be the best sex of my life.* This idea wasn't as shocking as it should have been. Cole was far gone. Far, far gone.

Hank took his time, curled over his lover, stroking his face and arms with his free hand. Cole rocked against him, nipping his throat, asserting himself. Hank's wide chest and panting belly were becoming more than he could stand.

"I'm ready, Hank. I'm so ready," Cole said.

Hank grunted in agreement, slathering the lube onto his cock with shaking fingers and nestled the head against Cole's opening.

"Hank," Cole breathed. "Yes." The word itself all he wanted to say. *Yes, Hank, yes.*

"I got you, baby," Hank said through clenched teeth and pushed forward. Cole bit back a cry and focused inward, willed his body to soften. Hank's soft tip eased through the tight ring, carefully, slowly.

Cole concentrated, staring somewhere in the middle space between them. Stars blew in his vision as his opening spread, taking his breath straight out of his lungs. His opening convulsed, swallowing the head of Hank's prick in one burning push.

"That's it," Hank said gently. "Let me in."

"Feels good," Cole said. "Goddamn, it's been a long time though."

His breathing was ragged, and little hitching moans kept bursting through his lips. Almost too soon Hank was fully seated, his solid warmth covering Cole, elbows bracketing his head.

"Now," he said softly. "You good?"

Cole swallowed and closed his eyes. He took a deep breath and let it all out, opening his eyes again. "Yeah," he said. "You feel amazing. Go slow though, okay?"

Hank rumbled in approval and began to rock his hips, sliding only a few inches in and out. Hank wanted to pound Cole into the bed—Cole could feel his shivering anticipation. But he was generous, to give Cole time, pushed up to his hands to angle himself so the little rough patch of Cole's prostate scraped along the top of his shaft. He did it again and again, painting Cole's inner vision with constellations until Cole thrashed his head against the sheets, deep grunts squeezed out of him with every push.

"Stroke yourself," Hank said. Grabbing Cole's legs under his knees, he forced them farther apart. It also had the effect of pinning Hank's cock against Cole's prostate. Cole's cock leaked everywhere as he stroked himself, twisting his wrist up under the head. Hank was staring, gaze greedy and reckless. He blinked when Cole caught him.

"Like what you see?" Cole asked, slowing down and pushing his cock to point at Hank's face.

"Promise you gonna be gentle with that thing later?"

"Of course," Cole said. "You can go harder now, by the way. I feel — Jesus, I'm closer than I thought."

"Yes, sir." Hank laughed and braced hard on his hands, flicking his gaze between Cole's face and his hand on his cock.

His hips snapped up and in. And again, hard and rough. Cole, undaunted, grabbed the headboard above his head to steady himself, taking it, even shoving back. He came with a breathless sigh, legs wrapped tight around Hank's waist.

His channel squeezed Hank, hard as a fist, glorious rippling pulls that tore Hank's own orgasm up from his hips. He barked out a surprised shout, screwing his hips in close, his mouth closing over Cole's. The kiss was messy and desperate and perfect. So perfect.

Hank pulled out, kicking over the table with the lamp and cups as he tipped over to Cole's side.

"Good thing the light's battery powered," Cole mumbled. Hank could barely catch his breath to laugh and pulled off the condom to roll against Cole's side.

"Goddamn, baby," he said. "You are something else."

They snuggled down, smiling into their kisses. It wasn't that late, and Cole had a feeling there would be another round or two before they were done. He let himself doze, contentment and anticipation tangling in his gut.

Chapter Fifteen

Hank

Hank wasn't sure if he could point to a single happier night. They ate the food he'd prepared as a midnight snack, kissing every chance they got, lying back to watch shooting stars and kissing some more. They talked about asteroids and how *The Expanse* was a criminally under-appreciated show. Cole talked animatedly, describing painting the orange stones and velvet stars. How clearly he saw it. He talked about the colors of fire while Hank took care of the dishes.

"This will get them clean enough not to be gross by the time my friend gets back here," Hank said, scrubbing their metal plates with sand. He flat refused Cole's help, asking about colors instead.

"This is your meeting," Cole said. "But this is the best night I've ever had. I feel like I owe you one."

"Does that mean I can play with your cock?" Hank asked over his shoulder with a grin. Cole laughed and yanked Hank to his feet, hard up against him.

"Absolutely," he said, nuzzling at Hank's neck. "It's yours for the taking."

Hank pushed Cole back a step and sank slowly to his knees, holding Cole's gaze. He paused in front of Cole's straining zipper and opened his mouth, waiting. The firelight danced over his face, showing the dimple through his beard, the mischief in his hazel eyes.

"Oh God, you're killing me," Cole said, fumbling his cock and balls out of his pants. Hank's face was nothing but anticipation and lust, a side of him that sent Cole's heart up into his throat. "You are full of surprises, Hank Ashton."

"That's the idea."

Cole gave himself a few strokes and squeezed the tip. A thick drop of precum oozed out and slid down into a long glistening string, shining in the firelight. Hank caught it on his tongue and followed it to the head of Cole's prick. Salt of the sea and bitter, he swallowed Cole down, eyes sliding closed, and hummed happily.

"Please," he said, reaching out and stroking Cole's thigh. "Let me do this for you, Cole."

Cole made a faint choking sound as Hank swallowed the head and first few inches of Cole's shaft in a long slide. Even though his lips were stretched wide, he still managed a little smile.

Cole stroked Hank's shaved scalp, groaning loudly, incoherent endearments and curses falling from his lips.

"How is it you are so good at this, gorgeous?" Cole gasped, running a thumb over Hank's swollen lips. Hank pulled back, kissing the tip of Cole's prick.

"Why does everyone assume I ain't had fun?" Hank said with a wicked grin. "I was twenty once, you know. And a fucking US Navy seaman."

He sounded stern, but Cole laughed. "I bet you were a hateful little twink," he said, tilting his hips. He squeezed the head of his cock again, feeding the stream of precum into Hank's open mouth.

Hank didn't say anything, lapping at the head of Cole's prick. But he winked, hoping Cole could picture it. Young Hank, a sailor, dark-haired, dimpled and a giant pain in his chief's ass. Cole tugged him to his feet so they could kiss more, hands roving under shirts and inside jeans, getting desperate.

"I am going to pound you into the mattress," Cole said breathlessly. "Is that okay? Can I? Pay you back?"

Hank moaned and ground his hips against Cole's. "I want it," he said, his voice rough. "Been thinking about this all week."

He couldn't name the emotions that were building up in him — something like joy, but also a strange grief at his previous loneliness — unacknowledged until now. He wanted this. Trusted Cole. The idea that there was no dominance or submission — that they were two men who could make each other happy, give each other whatever they needed without loss of… What exactly? He didn't care. *I'm a vers, he's a vers and we are going to have a good time while we can.*

"Come on then, sailor," Cole said. "Let's go back inside where we can fall asleep when we're done."

Inhibitions and worries had been shed the first time, so now they went straight for what they wanted. Cole on top, pushy, no longer worrying about how he looked. Hank was boneless, still rumbling sweet nothings, but making less sense, his eyes heavy-lidded. Cole's fingers made him shudder, made it hard to move, to even lift his hands. He wasn't wasting time, opening Hank purposefully, kissing the very breath out of him, searching deep with probing fingers. *Forgot how good that is. Someone else's hand, stretching… Fuck his fingers are thick.*

Moving slowly, much as they did under water, he let Cole position him as he wanted. Cole murmured indistinctly, keeping his body pressed against Hank even as he turned him onto his knees. He folded Hank over, chest on the bed, and put a firm hand between his shoulder blades, making him arch his back all the way. Slowly Cole pushed at Hank's arms until they were stretched out in front of him.

"Grab the bars of the headboard," he murmured. "Don't let go."

Cole's fingers were back in his opening, three and four, twisting and tugging at his rim. Hank choked out a curse, and Cole bent over him without withdrawing his fingers.

"Still good?" he whispered.

Hank nodded but didn't care—he was too far gone. His whole body was loose and open, ready. Another groan escaped his lips, and he ground his hips back against Cole's hand. When the fingers withdrew, Hank shivered, listening to Cole unrolling the condom.

"Please, Cole. I'm ready. I'm so fuckin' ready, baby."

"Shhhhhhh," Cole crooned, curving his body over Hank's. "I have you. I'm here."

Hank nodded and felt the first hard nudge at his opening. Grabbing the blanket between his teeth, he fought back the sounds he wanted to make. *Jesus, you are falling apart like nothing here.*

Hank was breathing hard through his nose, but he nodded again, making little thrusts back against the head of Cole's cock as it breached his hole, pulling him open. *God, that feels good — I'm gonna hurt tomorrow.*

Hank cried out again, muffled by the blanket in his teeth. At first, the stretch was torture, a fire blazing in his opening, his thighs, his hips. But the pain was nothing to the pleasure. Hank's cock dripped steadily, and Cole's shaft mashed his swollen prostate as it filled him, sliding in so slowly Hank wanted to scream.

"Oh, Hank, what are you doing to me?" Cole choked out, finally sinking forward until his hips were pressed against Hank's ass. "Goddamn, what are you doing to me?" he repeated, his breath ragged against Hank's back. He began to thrust slowly, grinding his hips in little circles. "You're like silk, Hank, so soft for me…"

Hank clenched his jaw. Cole was so deep it took his breath. Hank's body responded, his sense of self that he was always worrying about—the feeling that he had to be in charge, carefully aloof, apart, always right—all slipping away. It felt like freedom, like putting down a burden, letting go of old pain.

"Fuck me, Cole," he gasped. "Make me take it. I can take it, please, just…fuck me."

Cole laughed little puffs of air against Hank's back.

"Yes, sir," he said. He straightened up and snapped his hips hard.

Hank grunted but pushed back, a harsh *yes* bursting from his clenched teeth. A rhythm built between them, short shoving strokes, a pace set for climax—a rush between the press of Cole inside him and the gorgeous friction on his hole. *God, he is deep. So deep. Hurts good. I'm close.*

He pushed stuttering fingers against his belly, almost expecting to feel Cole there, and cupped his navel where the deepest burn was. Hank's thoughts were pops of light across a roaring dark sea of lust, building fast and hard.

Still braced against the heavy wood frame, he slid one hand between his legs and began stroking in time with Cole's thrusts. Hank's orgasm was coming in hot, the loosening of his thighs balanced against the tightening coil in his belly.

"Cole, damnit, Cole! I'm gonna come…" he said, his voice hitching. His knuckles were white where he gripped the headboard, his arm braced to take the force of Cole's hips. But his control was slipping fast. *I can't do this for much longer… I'm going to come so hard…*

The pleasure flooded up his spine, drowning him, taking his breath, rushing into every available space inside him. All he could feel was the spasming of Cole's cock, so deep it bordered on pain, huge in his gut. Then that was gone too, swallowed in the wave, and Hank's breath returning for one bellowing shout. He filled his palm in hot splashes, pulse after pulse.

When Cole pulled free, Hank collapsed forward, relief tangling with the emptiness in his core. He shuddered. The wave receded slowly. After ditching the condom, Cole tried to move to the side but that wasn't allowed. Absolutely not.

"Lie on me, Cole," Hank said, his voice a slurred rasp.

"I'm not too heavy?"

"Course not. Warm. Soft." The idea that Cole would not be covering every single inch of him was unacceptable. Not after so long alone.

What did you expect? You haven't had your bell rung out like that in…how long? He whined as Cole stirred and found himself fighting back tears. *I needed this more than I thought…as touch starved as I was. Jesus where did all these feelings come from? This is going to be a problem…*

But then, oh perfection, Cole draped over his back, arms wrapping his shoulders, straddling Hank's hips. Yes, he was heavy. That was the whole point. The pressure slowed every bit of rattling worry in his mind, shifting the gears down to a steady hum that faded, faded, and was gone.

Chapter Sixteen

Cole

Dawn. Cole's eyes slid open, and he regarded the man sprawled on his chest. Hank was snoring softly, his body loose and relaxed. *We switched places sometime during the night. God, I didn't even wake up.* Cole ran a hand along the smooth scalp and down Hank's face. Cole's body was singing to him, a discordant mix of ache and pleasure. Hank's massage had done wonders but afterward?

"Mmmphmm?" Hank made a small grumbling noise and shifted even further, curling his body so his face was buried in Cole's armpit. After a moment, the little purring snore returned, and Cole shook his head, joy twisting his heart.

The sky was gray in the east, the stars fading in the growing blue. And he had to piss something fierce. But Hank's body felt good draped over him...a conundrum.

Hank shifted again and made an incoherent mumble before lifting his head, blinking at Cole in confusion.

"Is it morning?" he asked, his voice scratchy and hoarse. He looked around at the mess of the tent and a smile chased across his handsome face. "God, what a night!" He leaned in for a kiss. "Coffee?"

Cole caught a yawn and struggled to sit up as well.

"Yes, please. As strong as you can make it."

"Good man," Hank said, waving a thumbs-up as he staggered out of the tent.

Bodily needs met, coffee in hand, they sat side by side on a stone, watching the light shift over the hills and cliffs across the valley. The colors stole Cole's breath. With a blanket around them, he and Hank amused themselves by swallowing mouthfuls of hot coffee and blowing foggy breaths, the moisture immediately sucked out of the air.

"Damn, I'm sore. But good sore!" Hank added when he obviously saw Cole's worry.

"Me too," Cole said. "Good sore. Last night was... It was great. It was amazing."

"Yeah," Hank agreed, sipping his coffee. "Can I confess something?"

"With this view? This coffee? After last night?" Cole laughed. "Of course."

"I'm a little worried." Hank addressed his worry to his coffee cup, shoulders bunched. "My feelings have already been...kind of running away with me."

Relief washed over Cole, and he bumped Hank's forehead with his.

"God, me too," he said. "I don't even know what to think anymore."

"I think," Hank said hesitantly, "that if we were in another setting, we'd be dating, and I'd be telling my mama about you."

Cole took this in, his mind scouring for solutions. He could come back. Of course. Book a different hotel? Would that be enough? But Hank lived in this town — he had a reputation to maintain. He couldn't get in trouble. And Cole — well, Embassy personnel were strongly, *very* strongly, counseled against this kind of relationship in country.

Again the end of their affair loomed, and again Cole pushed it away.

"I don't know what to do," he said. "But yeah. I think... I think we're in trouble."

* * * *

"This is your apartment?" Cole looked around in amazement. The drive home had been somber, Cole mostly worrying about their situation, scrolling through a host of impossible scenarios. Before he knew it, he was following Hank up a set of wide stone stairs, carrying both their backpacks, since Hank carried their supplies.

"Yeah? Why?" Hank asked over the top of the boxes. He set them on the counter and took the bags from Cole's arms.

"It's gorgeous."

"Where did you think I lived?" Hank laughed. He set about unpacking, putting dirty dishes to one side, leftover food in the fridge.

"The way you talk, I figured some little rat hole above a falafel shop."

"Nah, the falafel place is two doors down."

Hank's apartment was on the top floor, and Cole's mind had conjured a cramped little space. Instead, white stucco'd walls soared up at an angle with exposed rafters. The living room wasn't large, but the high ceiling and wide windows gave a sense of airy space. The floors throughout were tiled in swirling white stone, with colorful rugs thrown where needed. A bedroom Cole only peeked into, seeing a large, neatly made bed and a huge wardrobe, had an exposed stone wall on one side and art hanging on the other two.

The kitchen was small, a galley, made tolerable by another big window. Hank had it open now, letting the breeze blow in as he washed dishes.

"Here let me help," Cole said. Hank pointed to a dish towel hanging on a wooden rack and Cole stood shoulder to shoulder with him, the two washing, drying and stacking. Before long they were on Hank's tiled balcony, overlooking the mountains behind the town.

"There's another little balcony off the bedroom that faces the water," Hank said. "This is more private, but I used to drink my coffee out there—wave to all my neighbors on the street. You can just see the tourist area if you crane your neck. Good for people watching."

"How many apartments in this building?"

"About a dozen or so."

"God, my apartment in Cairo would fit in your bedroom. And my only view is the wall across the alley and the old man who pisses on it every morning."

"That sounds terrific. Just super. Real nice." Hank laughed. "I think I'd shrivel up and die."

"You would. Can't even keep a houseplant alive in there. There's no sun. But at least it isn't hot. It has AC and a few other ex-pats mixed in."

"Damn, I thought you all lived in nice houses."

"No," Cole said ruefully. "Or maybe senior staff does. But I'm a very small fish. I get the dark box facing the piss wall."

"Can't you move?"

"I'm making it sound worse than it is." Cole laughed, stretching his arms overhead and breathing deep. "I love my job. And I love my neighbors. The old lady next door always makes extra food if I'm coming in late. And I play rugby in the park on the corner. But this…" He waved to the mountains, shining in the heat. "You must have nice sunsets."

"I'm usually home after they happen," Hank said. He pivoted slowly, looking at the mountains. "But yeah. You're right. It's a hell of a view."

Cole wanted to kiss him but restrained himself. Last night was still fresh. His groin ached. He both wanted more and wanted to sleep for days. He watched Hank poring over his hand drawn map, deciding their next dive, admiring the back of Hank's neck, the terrible tattoos marching around his muscular —

"I'd better go, baby," Cole said.

"All right," Hank answered without looking up. "I'll see you at the shop tomorrow."

Before temptation could really get its claws in, Cole made his way through a side entrance and headed to the nearest café. He'd spend a few hours smoking hookah and talking with the woodcarvers. Then back to the Grande like nothing had happened, for a shower and sweet, sweet sleep.

Tomorrow they could do it all again.

* * * *

Loading the golf cart the next day, they could barely look at each other. Cole was sure his ears were on fire. Hank was in full grumpy grouper mode, but the corner of his mouth kept twitching. They barely managed to get to the boat without incident.

One thing Cole appreciated, despite the butterflies flailing in his gut — Hank was incredibly serious about their dives. It would have taken very little to convince Cole to skip the dives and fuck all morning like a teenager. If this had just been a casual class — the basics Cole saw Hank teaching in the afternoons sometimes — it wouldn't matter.

But the dives were more than that. Each one was a gift. Hank sharing a part of himself with Cole. They had become a kind of love language.

Cole's mind skittered away from that word. *I mean just as like – this is a thing we share. Not love love – but this is an experience we are doing together.*

Today they were back at the column of light rockfall. This time they motored close to the cliff face so Hank could show Cole how the rocks had tumbled. The sunlight on the red stone face had Cole hanging over the edge of the boat, taking photos upwards, sideways. He made Hank steer them to different spots so he could sketch and snap more photos for later. Hank encouraged him, pointing out features.

By the time they went under the water, it was a different world. The shaft of light, which had so entranced Cole their first time here, was gone, replaced by a diffused glow. The water above the rock fall was a soft gold, bouncing off the face of the stone like a photographer's reflector. Multi-dimensional light, shining from two directions, eliminated shadows and doubled shapes. As clear as the water was, the effect was transcendent. *I thought we were flying before. But now you can't even see the water.* Through the camera, his slow pivots looked like drone footage over a forest, swaying in the wind.

Cole turned himself in a slow circle, taking photos to remind himself later. How to paint something like this? How to even begin? Hank hovered in the water below and to his right, arms crossed, relaxed, head tilted as he looked around. The reef fish didn't mind his presence, carrying on with their business. A large silver and blue one cruised close to peer at Hank's tank before moving on.

It's like he's part of the reef. Just another fish hanging out. I wish he was this relaxed out of the water.

Cole looked up again, giving a lazy kick to move around a large stone. In the double light it looked square, once Cole accounted for the growth of coral and other...

No. It *was* square. Cole drifted to the other side. Square. He turned back again. It was definitely square. And now that he looked — so was another stone, buried beneath, but illuminated now by the glow reflected off the cliff.

He fumbled for Hank, hovering behind, and caught his wrist, pulled him forward. Remembering the hand signals they'd practiced —

I see — look there —

Question?

Cole described the shape with his hands. Hank tilted his head left and right then did what Cole had, rolled sideways to see the other stone below. When he looked back, his eyes were wide.

I see — swim — look — okay.

Okay.

They moved slowly, careful not to touch the coral or disturb the creatures that lived there. Hank was able to maneuver into the smallest spaces, perfectly still, holding a hand to certain stones for Cole to photograph the scale. At three hundred psi, they came to the surface, clambering wordlessly onto the boat again.

"My log will be ridiculous." Cole laughed. "I don't think we were below twenty feet the whole time."

"Twenty-four feet was your max." Hank tapped his dive computer. "Let's draw the layout while it's fresh. We have two more tanks each."

They tried not to drip on Cole's sketchbook. Hank fed Cole mouthfuls of eggs and potatoes while he worked, and if he slipped a few kisses in, well, Cole did not object. They managed a rough sketch, guessing distances.

"Okay, so we aren't crazy," Cole said. "There were six blocks."

"And two columns."

"That can't be right."

"Calling me a liar?" Hank's eyes were slits of happiness. Impulsively, Cole leaned over and kissed his cheek. Hank ducked his head and pushed his shoulder into Cole's.

"Of course not. But how many times have you been here?"

"Don't remind me!" Hank threw his hands up. "That column of light only comes certain times so I been here on and off for a couple of years and I never even noticed them blocks."

"What about other divers?"

"I never brought anyone else to dive here," Hank muttered, jabbing at the eggs.

"I knew that grumpy grouper shit was an act." Cole laughed.

"Okay, I admit I wanted to impress you."

"It worked," Cole said. He pushed Hank's sunglasses up and kissed him, a quick press of lips, trying to put as much feeling into it as possible. A thrill of joy bubbled over and through him.

"You got me in knots, Cole," Hank said seriously. "Let's get under the water again before I jump on you and tip this boat over."

Chapter Seventeen

Hank

Hank was no stranger to kicking himself. But this was a spectacular miss. As he and Cole dropped down, looking at the rockfall from above this time, it was so damn obvious. Sure, most of the stones were boulders of varying shapes and sizes, but the angles of the blocks were clear, once he saw them. He could only blame himself. Or rather, he could thank Cole. Everything looked different since Cole.

He sees things like I should. I can't even see past my own pissed-off ego. If I could get out from under Khaled, I'd be so good to him. Make sure he got to make all the art he wants. Take him everywhere, show him the whole Sea.

Cole hovered, legs crossed to keep his fins off the reef, like a floating buddha, rubbing his chin and looking around him. Hank's heart twisted hard and mean in his chest. *He's so sure in his body when he isn't thinking about it. God, I want to roll him in bed so bad.*

Suddenly Cole flipped over, darting away with a couple of strong kicks, turning sideways and making for a jumble of broken coral on a stone shelf. Hank followed, caught by Cole's urgency. Cole hung upside down, his face inches from the rubble before frantically waving Hank over.

Something *gleamed*, the barest shine, only catching the light because it was so beautifully reflected off the cliff face. But that light faded as fast as the sun rose. How had Cole even seen it?

Cole looked to him, hovering his finger above to the little patch of shine. It was only a few inches across, covered in sand and broken coral and one live fan, stretching bravely to the sun. Hank nodded.

Watch me.

He drew his dive knife and studied the live coral. It grew on a broken chunk, and there were two tiny black fish in its honeycomb sides, looking out at them. Hank slid his knife under the broken piece and lifted the entire thing, with its coral house and residents, up to the next level of the ledge, where the light was the same. He placed it with the care he would a sleeping baby and when he looked back, Cole grinned widely behind his mouthpiece.

I see you.

Hank flicked Cole's ear in reply, bumped their masks together. They moved the pieces of broken dead coral one by one, taking photos as they went. Hank removed the sand by waving hard above it, pushing with the water. When it had drifted away, he froze, only breathing out of habit, his heart beating like the surf on the cliffs. Cole hovered by him, camera forgotten in his hands, eyes as wide as Hank's felt.

Gold. Its shape so familiar. Hank's brain immediately conjured the cheap reproductions available in every stall of the market. *It can't be real. It can't. It can't.*

Cole touched it first, his finger tracing the curved beak, the upraised wing. A falcon—*the* falcon. *Horus.* Not as elaborate as the enameled one from Tutankhamen's treasure, this one was plain gold, the size of a dinner plate. One wing was broken off, but there was no mistaking it. It was nearly featureless, only the red disc of the sun on its head still in place.

Hank's dive computer blipped, and he saw he had sucked half his tank in his excitement. He caught Cole's attention.

This time they didn't speak on the surface. Hank set a timer for the surface interval, and they cleared all their gear into the corners, under the benches. Cole sketched his photos quickly and efficiently between bottles of water.

They sacrificed his plastic food container, putting it in the loose string bag Hank used to pick trash off the reef. They shed every piece of gear they didn't need. They were going down with one task and one task only.

The falcon fit perfectly in the plastic tub. It was solid, heavy even in the water. Hank cradled the tub in his arms, maintaining good dive discipline despite his pounding heart. *It can't be real. It can't be. Maybe it's gold. Maybe. But it's probably some souvenir from the nineteen-hundreds. It can't be real. It can't.*

His dive shop, his own place, specializing in marine life, in geology and archeology. Working only with private divers, the real deal. No more basic classes—ever.

He refused to let the idea form. Couldn't get his hopes up. The falcon couldn't be real. It couldn't.

"It's real," Cole said, his face practically in the tub. The boat rocked gently in the silence that followed, the sounds of waves slapping the hull in perfect match to Hank's pounding heart. The falcon gleamed dully in its container. They didn't dare take it out of the water, unsure what would happen in the air. It looked like what it was—a crusty, muddy lump, with a golden wing. How?

"What do you mean?" Hank asked. The question came out as a strangled bark, and Cole shot him a reproachful look. "Sorry, baby. I'm a little freaked out here."

"I mean it's real gold."

"How old is it?"

"I'm not sure. Old. Really fucking old."

"Like…Napoleonic war souvenir old?"

Cole's face was solemn, his eyes shining. "Like old, old. Way old. Really fucking old. All I can tell is it's more than a thousand years. But I can't tell if it's ancient, like Ramses-type stuff. But the way it's made — it's molded, in beeswax—I think they did that in the intermediate period. I need to look up some stuff."

"Jesus," Hank breathed. The vision of his dive shop trembled like a mirage, almost real, almost. "So even if it's not ancient Egypt, it's still—"

"Really damn old." Cole put the lid on the plastic tub and tucked it under the bench, wedged between their gear to hold it steady, and out of the sun. "I can't even look at it right now. Look at my hands!"

Hank knelt down, taking Cole's trembling hands and kissing each knuckle, turning them and pressing his lips into Cole's palms. "What happens now?" he asked.

Cole tugged him forward into a hug. "We need to do a bunch of research. And we need to think about next steps. But honestly? Right now, I just want to be in this moment."

Hank pulled back, cupped Cole's round cheeks. "Let's go back. You can come to my place, okay?"

"Okay," Cole said. "Let's take Horus back. Better keep it quiet. I'll grab my laptop from my room."

They cleaned their gear in grim silence, both lost in thought. Whenever their eyes met, Hank's helpless smile felt suspicious, too bright for teacher and student. He kept his eyes fixed on the small, mundane tasks before them. Cole sat in the front seat of the truck, clutching his laptop and sketchbook to his chest like life preservers. Hank felt the same way, his grip on the steering wheel hard enough to bruise.

The tub, towels thrown over the top, sat between them, untouched the whole ride into town.

This would be the discovery of Cole's career. If it was real, presenting it to the Antiquities Ministry was the main task, to ensure the site was preserved and every possible artifact cataloged and brought up. He held his breath as they bounced along the rutted track to the road, refusing to look at the tub beside him.

If it was a site, Hank could lead those dives. The idea sent a jolt of excitement through him. *It could launch his dive shop, maybe. Either way, when we open the exhibit, he'll get co-discovery credit. One of those 'on behalf of the Egyptian people' plaques. Our names in the history books if it really is a temple.*

The rutted track finally gave way to gravel, too loud for talk to be possible. He and Hank shared a nervous grin but no more.

My God, what if it's another of these sunken palaces? What an exhibit it will make. It will bring people from all over to see it! Maybe there can be a smaller exhibit here? Connect this area so the tourists come back? The Egyptians are going to be thrilled. And the Brits will be so pissed.

Cole thought of Lord Fawlter, the British Antiquities Liaison. Bastard. His entire purpose was to stonewall the Egyptians from getting their own history back. Not that the Smithsonian had much of a leg to stand on. But Cole was firmly on Team Repatriation and had led several initiatives to return items. *After my paper, finding something special like this and handing it over, all in public? Ambassador Jenks will have a field day.*

He daydreamed the whole drive down the beach road. He didn't think he could ever get enough of the red brown hills between blue sky and blue sea. Or the nestle of colorful shops and houses of Al'Shahin itself.

When the Antiquities people take over the site, maybe they will let me stay, be a kind of liaison. We might even be allowed to dive the site together – as observers or something. I could see Hank whenever he wanted. And see the artists here. Paint again.

Hank's neighbors were used to him clunking up and down stairs with gear. And since he was considerate about it, quiet during prayers and when everyone slept, no one seemed to care about him wrestling a sloshing box of water up the narrow stairs, Cole following along with his usual equipment. Nader even helped them, carrying the empty lunch boxes to Hank's door. He paid no mind to the tub, or the towels thrown over it.

Inside his apartment, Hank put the tub with the falcon on his coffee table—didn't even look at it. Some superstitious part of him thought if he looked at it, he would somehow see, in the rational afternoon light, that it was fake, the whole thing a dream. *Don't wanna jinx it. Just put it away. We'll deal later.*

"Let me get food started, okay?"

"Yeah," Cole said absently. He was pulling clothes out of his bag, eyes dreamy. They sharpened on Hank. "Can I admit I'm scared to even open it?"

Hank gave a relieved nod. *Yes. God yes.*

"Go shower," Hank said. "Towels are in the cabinet. Let's not even talk about the thing until we have a little food in us."

The falcon never left his mind. He chopped vegetables dreaming of the Horus, careful to frame his thoughts so as to neither get his hopes up nor invite bad luck. He was a sailor to the core in that respect, giving the wooden cutting board a sharp knock with his knuckles.

Wiping his hands off with a towel, he shivered. Really real, not only the gold, but the age of it—if it was a real ancient artifact? Well then. If that were the case, and there was no harm in a little fantasizing, surely.

If it's real, then... I sell it to Samir's buddy—the Algerian. Antiquity like that? On the black market it would fetch a million. Me and Cole could get a hundred grand each. Enough that my half would set me up for life. Cole could have his own gallery. Me and him could see each other whenever we wanted.

Chapter Eighteen

Hank

"I convinced myself it was fake," Hank said. "But now looking at it…"

They had widened the small, exposed portion with a washcloth, still in the seawater, enough to see the dark mellow shine of gold.

"These things are a dime a dozen in the market," Hank continued. "That chest piece of King Tut's — but this. This's different. Even my himbo ass can tell."

"You have an excellent himbo ass. But yeah, the gold is real," Cole agreed. "And it isn't gold leaf. That's the strange part. The ancients were rock stars about gold leaf. This is solid, though. They shaped solid gold like this in beeswax molds."

"How?" Hank asked. He supposed part of him cared. But the litany of *It's real, It's real, It's real* in his head was louder than anything else. Still trying not to get ahead of himself — he had looked up the current rate for gold, and a kilo, which felt like a conservative number for the falcon, was around fifty thousand dollars. He only owed Khaled fifteen.

"I could give you a thirty-slide presentation on paper-making in the ancient world, but I don't know shit about gold," Cole said absently, gently rubbing a small section over the red sun. "This enamel work—I'd better leave it alone. Another expert I need."

"I know a couple of people we could ask," Hank agreed. "But probably shouldn't until we are ready to sell, otherwise they'll rip us off blind."

Cole froze, turning to Hank with a frown. "What?"

"The guys I know, wouldn't want to give them any—"

"What do you mean sell?"

"The falcon? How much do you think it weighs?"

"Sell it?" Cole asked. The look of dawning outrage on his face stopped Hank in his mental tracks. "Sell it? Are you crazy? What do you mean sell it?"

Hank didn't understand. Cole's incredulity, his anger, was totally unfeigned. But Hank really didn't understand. He had been working off the basis of evaluating the falcon for sale for the last eight hours. He didn't have any room in his head for another idea. And Cole's face made it clear he was nowhere near on the same page. Whatever Hank had been thinking—he and Cole—

"Of course sell it." He laughed, confusion cracking his voice. "What else would we do with it? A solid gold paperweight?"

Cole sat back in the chair with a grunt. The washcloth dripped unnoticed onto his jeans. The realization dawned on Hank—they were not thinking the same thing. Not even close.

"If you're kidding, you need to stop," Cole said seriously. "This belongs in a museum. We have to turn it over to the government. They have to evaluate the site. There could be more—"

"The government?" Hank took a step back, his fists clenching, trying to hold on to the last shred of before, of where they had been ten minutes ago when Hank had thought they were together on this. His shop, his debt? No. Impossible. The ringing in his ears made him drop into the other chair. "We can't give this to the *government*."

"We can, and we have to." Cole's voice rose along with his chin. "You can't seriously suggest we sell this? To who?"

"I know a guy—"

"You *know a guy*? You're talking black market? You're talking about *stealing*."

"We found it! It ain't stealing! We found it!"

"It doesn't belong to us!"

"What the fuck are you talking about?"

"What the fuck are *you* talking about?" Cole shot to his feet, standing over the falcon, glaring down at Hank. "You're talking about theft. About smuggling. Looting!"

"You gotta be kidding me?" Hank's neck burned, his throat rough from shouting. "You know how much crap they dig up outta here every year? This country has plenty of gold falcons! Why do they need this one?"

"I can't believe this." Cole threw his hands up, realized he had the washcloth and dropped it onto the box with a splat. His finger shook, pointing at Hank. "You can't be saying this!"

"Me?" Hank bellowed. The chair arms were digging into his palms. He felt like he could rip them off with the slightest pressure. "How can you take something, something the sea gave us — something we found together — and just hand it over to the Egyptians?"

"How can you take a discovery like this and turn it into some disgusting transaction?" Cole shot back. "That site! This could be the find of the decade! It could be a palace! It will bring tourists, scientists, archeologists from everywhere! The town will —"

"We can tell them about the site," Hank said eagerly. He scooted to the front of the chair, holding his hands up to Cole, trying to catch his fingers. "We can sell the Horus. But still tell them. I bet they'll find all kind of things. And we can keep this one!"

"No." Cole's tone was final. "I won't be a part of that. I won't be another foreigner stealing shit. That's immoral. Do you know what — ?"

Hank surged to his feet.

"Fuck your morals!" The shout tore his throat. "I *need* the money, Cole! I need the fucking money! I'll never get out of here! I owe a gangster fifteen thousand dollars! Why do you think I work at that hotel? Why do you think I don't have my own shop? At this rate I'll be his fucking slave for another decade! I need this fucking money. *Please*, Cole!"

Cole drew back. His chin came up, face going as carefully neutral as he had in front of Khaled. Hank loomed over him, heart thundering, breaking, shattering at Cole's obvious disgust. *Me. He's disgusted with me. After everything we been through.*

"Don't look at me like that," Hank begged. He couldn't bear it, turned his head away. *I ain't no better than his ex. Shouting at him.* "I'm sorry."

Hank dropped into the chair, his face in his hands. "Jesus Christ — I never thought. Even for a second —

that we weren't on the same page." How could this be happening? How could Cole possibly be so stubborn? "But we gotta sell it. It will set you up too, don't you see?"

"If you really thought I could do that?" Cole said, his voice low, condemning. "You don't understand me at all."

"Obviously," Hank said dully. He was a million miles away, entire halls of doors slamming closed in his mind *thump thump thump*, slamming closed in his heart, as shut off as it had been when he first met Cole. When the last door closed, he could speak. "What now?"

"Why didn't you tell me?" Cole demanded. Hank gave a bitter snort of laughter.

"Oh hey, hot guy, wanna be with a loser with a mob debt and a shitty dead-end job? That keeps me stuck in a dead town being yelled at by co-eds half my age? Of course I didn't tell you! I wanted... I wanted you to *like* me."

"But—"

"I think you should leave," Hank said. How could this hurt so much? "Take your treasure and go."

"I'm leaving, but you can keep the falcon."

"What?" Hank looked up, disbelieving. Really? Cole's face was closed shut, his eyes shining with tears, his expression a dagger through Hank's heart.

"Keep it," Cole said bitterly. "Keep the falcon. You can do whatever you want with it. I'm going back to Cairo. I'll wait two weeks before I tell them about the site."

"What about your high and mighty—?"

"Shut the fuck up, you selfish asshole," Cole snapped. "I won't have any part of the sale. Should be enough money for you to escape this supposed prison—this terrible, horrible prison. Run away, or whatever it is you want to do."

"Get out," Hank said, anger surging up again. "You got no idea what you're talking about."

"Apparently not," Cole said. "Apparently I don't know you at all."

Chapter Nineteen

Cole

Cole managed not to cry in the cab, nor when he threw all his stuff into his bag, stuffing the dive log in without a glance. He didn't cry when he checked out, refusing to answer any of the manager's confused questions.

Yes, the Grande had been excellent. No, he still needed to check out early. No, there was nothing they could do to get him to stay. Yes, he would be leaving a good review.

He didn't shed a single goddamn tear until he was in his apartment in Cairo, door closed and bags dumped on the floor. Then he stalked into the tiny dribbling shower and cried his fucking eyes out. He got takeout from the place on the corner on autopilot, climbing the stairs and locking himself in his apartment without being entirely sure how he did it. Two bites of food, two bites and he remembered the daily menus Hank made, the joy he had in revealing each recipe.

"This is hell," Cole said, startling himself. "How is this possible? How the hell is this possible?" Every dream, plan, half-assed idea he'd had for them to be together. It was laughable now. No reward from the government would include paying off a debt to a gangster. They'd cut him out of every connection to the find. *Too unsavory of a story.* "That's who that slimy guy in the white shirt was. I bet anything. Poor Hank. Fucking asshole! Why didn't he tell me?"

He ignored the pachinko parlor sound effects of notifications swirling into his work phone. *I'll go back to the office early, I guess? No. I need to fucking wallow. I have five more days. Fuck. I need to call Elia and Laura.*

"I'm back in Cairo," Cole started, once he'd connected. He couldn't even wrap his brain around explaining the whole thing. But he was determined not to cry. That much he could resolve.

"What?" Elia asked, leaning in. "Already?"

"I had a big fight with Hank and I came back." Their dismay made his resolve crumble. "I can't tell you any of the details, but it was rough."

"Did he hurt you?" Laura snapped. "Say one word, and I'll have him on a rendition list by tomorrow morning." Her eyes filled almost the whole screen, as if she could see Hank in the background.

"You're awful," Cole said, giving a shaky laugh. It felt good to have people so completely, even radically, on his side. "No, it just turned out we had opposing views on things that really matter to me, and I am very fucking sad right now."

"Oh, honey," Elia said. "I am so sorry."

There was some good news at least. "On the plus side—we made a discovery," he said. "You will hear about it if it pans out."

"What kind of discovery?" Elia asked.

Cole told them the bare bones of the event, leaving out the Horus. "So it was obvious once we looked. It's a piece of a wall and some columns under a cliff face in the water."

"That's amazing," Laura said, filling the screen with applause emojis. "Oh, Cole, I hope it pans out! What a coup that would be for you. But is that what you and Hank fought about?"

"Sort of," Cole conceded. "I don't want to think about it too hard. He's a good man. He is such a good man. But it turns out all this other stuff was going on I didn't know about. And like, okay, he didn't tell me because we only knew each other a week but I'm so hurt. I'm so hurt. We had this incredible night."

A clear vision of the two of them huddled under a blanket, watching the space station fly over made Cole cover his face with both hands. He barely heard the sympathies from his friends. "And I was thinking heavy thoughts. Like big, making it work despite everything thoughts. I really saw something there."

"What are you going to do now?" Elia asked gently.

That was the million-dollar question. What could he do to possibly take his mind off things? The answer was the same it had always been.

"I am going to throw myself into work, of course. It's busy as hell. I have a show to host. And then I will tell someone in Antiquities about the dive site, see if there is anything there."

"What about art?" Laura asked.

"Yeah..." Cole closed his eyes, tried to sense what that word meant. The break in his block, was it still true? Behind his tired lids, swirls of blue and green danced to life, deep and vibrant, sweeping his small apartment away. His hands twitched. "I think…I think maybe I'd better buy some more paint."

* * * *

Cole thought he had perfected the death-defying route to the embassy from his apartment. Cairo traffic was on a level he had never imagined. His first month in-country, he had nearly been killed twice. Not in a metaphorical way, but in the blasting heat of a minibus millimeters from his face, so close it slapped his head sideways way.

But over the two years he had mastered it, felt like he knew what he was doing as he dodged intersections and timed his crossings, raised hand palm-up, thumb and fingers touching, pulled downward in the universal Arabic gesture for 'wait' as he darted between dusty tuk-tuks and trucks and shining Mercedes.

This week had been like starting all over again. Square one. A noob, as the Marines said. The one on the gate had shouted a warning to save him from a swerving tuk-tuk. It took the whole gate process, from the outer security managed by the Egyptians, all the way to the Marine in the embassy proper, to still Cole's hammering heart.

"What's wrong, Cole?" the Marine asked. "You too distracted crossing that street. You can't exactly run, you know?" He gave Cole a sage nod, practically wagging his finger at his belly.

Cole snatched his badge back with a glare. *Twenty-one, peak fit, fat-phobic and dumb as a bag of rocks. Ignore him.*

"I mean..." The Marine started to back-pedal, seeing Cole's face.

"I get it," Cole snapped and hurried away before he said anything stupid.

The AC was out in his office, so he pried the window open, but closed it again when the smell of exhaust and cacophony of the street were too much. *Guess I'll just sweat. Fuck. Fuckity fuckums.* His mind veered to the sea breeze and heat of Al'Shahin. Hotter than Cairo, sure, but clean. And so of course to Hank. Hank steering the boat, sure handed and straight backed. Curling against Hank's chest, sketching. Hank's meals —

Nope. Nope. Nope. That selfish fuck. That ungrateful bastard. Bad enough he'll always be the first person who took me diving — that's enough right there. Cole had already booked another trip, to another coastal town, planning to get his Underwater Archeology certification. Nothing would keep him out of the water now. The idea that he might be diving with Hank again, at the site in Al'Shahin, diving and pretending not to care — well, that was a problem for future Cole. Right now, he was too busy to think about that.

"You are really out of it." The cultural attaché was ostensibly Cole's boss, though Leon gave Cole so much leeway it was more like a partnership. They were both on the Union board and both part of the LGBTQ alliance at the State Department. But that didn't mean Cole was willing to share his personal life. So he put a smile on his face, and forced out a chuckle.

"I hadn't had leave in a long time — I guess my brain is still trying to get back into the groove." *I shouldn't have left. I should have talked to him. If he really owes money to someone like that? I hope he can get out of it with the falcon. I can't blame him, but I wish I had stayed. Talked it out.*

"I have the same issue when I finish a good book," Leon said. "The regular world makes no sense for a few days."

"It's why I gave myself a couple weeks to finalize this event," Cole said, forcing his thoughts back to the present. "Instead of coming back a couple days before."

"Smart move."

"Do you know who the Antiquities Minister is bringing?" Cole asked. "I may do a little champagne diplomacy on the side."

"Let me look at the list."

Chapter Twenty

Hank

Hank made it a week before completely falling apart. He was at Leila's, playing cards, dreading her questions. She had kept her silence so far, watching him with shrewd eyes and snapping her cards down to convey her growing impatience.

"Yeah, I lost him," Hank said finally. "I fucking lost him, and it's only now beginning — I'm just now — I was stupid, Leila. I was really stupid."

He told her everything. The dives, the falcon, the night under the stars — the sense he had — the glimpse of their combined future…

"Oh, Hank, such heartbreak over something so foolish!"

"It's not foolish," Hank said, his head hanging between his shoulders, elbows braced on his knees. He wanted to cry but that seemed beyond him now. A dull pain thumped behind his eyes. His face was numb and his chest too tight to let any emotions pass through.

"Have you sold this falcon?"

"No. I can't even look at it."

"I see…"

"I mean, he said he would wait two weeks until he told anyone. It's been one week."

"And he works for the American Embassy?"

"Yeah, he does art exhibits for them."

"My poor dear," Leila said. "Hank, we have been friends for a long time now. Just as you took care of me when I broke my arm, I will take care of you."

The numbness gave way, thawed enough for him to give Leila a tired smile.

"Thanks, Leila, but this ain't lemon soup territory," he said.

She lay a hand on her breast, her dark eyes wide. "How dare you? Nothing is outside territory of lemon soup!"

* * * *

He walked home from Leila's slowly, lost in his own thoughts. The swinging lanterns and happy chatter around him sounded strange to his ears. He leaned against his usual wall, seeing the women on the patio again. They were in a tight huddle, a grandson with a laptop in their center. They all spoke at once, occasionally pointing at the screen and batting the poor boy on his shoulder in between sips of tea. Hank pushed off and forced his lead feet along to his apartment.

Sleep didn't come. He gave up on it around four and made coffee. *Might as well enjoy myself.* He arranged a couple of croissants, yogurt, half a melon—why not? Why not enjoy it? He sat on his front balcony, watching the sun rise. When was the last time he had done this? The sky faded to purple, to red, to rose, to blush like a flower petal.

Hank smiled, breathing in his coffee, counting the colors to himself as they appeared. He didn't know enough words for pink but he counted at least five different shades. The sun popped above the horizon, shooting gold in every direction — a glad shout of another burning day. His last croissant and coffee, he carried to the other balcony to see the colors on the hills as the sun touched their tips, stroking pink and orange fingers down their flanks.

"Everything is beautiful," he said. "My life may be a fucking disaster, but Cole's right — everything is beautiful here."

Hank decided then and there that he was going to watch every sunrise he possibly could. *And show a little gratitude. Take more time with my students.* More time meant fewer students, which meant less money. Hank found, watching the world come to burning life around him, that he didn't care about the fucking money. He was going to channel his inner Cole, and delight in his life.

* * * *

Hank's newest student settled down once she was in the water, looking around her with curiosity and a smile around her mouthpiece. She had been so nervous, seasick, a general mess. But private lessons were private lessons, and Hank was determined to focus on work. Focus and forget. Forget Cole, forget the falcon still in its tub under his bed. Forget the last three weeks had even happened.

Audrey was from Jerusalem, had fought off cancer and decided to catch up on things she had not done until now. Diving was at the top of her list. Something in his new breakfast ritual had mellowed Hank all week. So he was patient with Audrey, taking an extra day to snorkel with her, working on shallow dives with a portable tank, just to help her work on her buoyancy.

And now the reward was clear. They were on the same drift dive he had taken Cole to — *stop thinking about him. Just stop.* It was perfect for Audrey. Very little swimming — they could let the current sweep them gently through the reef. He cupped her elbow, enough to let her know he was close. She kept patting him on the shoulder, pointing at things, her eyes happy slits behind her mask.

The reef gifted them all sorts of creatures. Audrey clutched his arm when a nurse shark made its slow, sleepy way across the sand below them. A turtle rode the current with them for a time, and they even saw a sea serpent, black and white, undulating from one reef pile to another. Not wanting to be reminded of Cole, Hank turned them out of the current in a different place, taking Audrey to visit a few clown fish he knew.

But if the idea was not to think about Cole, he was failing. The truth? Everything made him think of Cole. And not just individual sights, but the entire feel of the water. The scales had fallen from his eyes indeed. Everything was vibrant and beautiful. Darting fish, the bubbles they sent spiraling up to the surface — it was a magical space.

And Audrey's delight, her delicate blue-veined hands clutched before her in joy as the turtle veered close to examine her, was cracking his shell as much as Cole had. Or rather, Cole had cracked the shell, and now as each piece fell away, Hank was left naked and vulnerable to the joys around him. Not wanting to fill his mask with snot, he pushed the emotions away and focused on his student.

"Oh, Hank," Audrey said, as they got back onto the boat. The other divemaster was gathering his students to the other boat, and their laughter carried over the glass-smooth sea. Audrey was on her toes, hands clasped. The joy shining through her eyes made Hank stand an inch taller.

"It was perfect," she continued. "It was the most beautiful thing. I never imagined. Thank you, thank you!"

"It was my pleasure," Hank said. "It's a beautiful day to be in the Sea. The water's like crystal. You rest while I switch your tank. Make sure you note the turtle in your log, and the sea snake. And if you peek in that icebox, you'll see I made us a nice spread."

They dug into their lunches, still talking, and Hank realized that here was another person who would dive lifelong. And she might not have, if he hadn't taken so much extra time with her. Guilt flushed his cheeks. *How many of those kids would have been like this, if I hadn't been such a son of a bitch? How many would have really gotten it, with a little patience? A little kindness? Cole was right.*

He took them the long way to the next site, showing Audrey the best views, and asking her about the geology. She had a surprising store of information about the plate tectonics of the region. Hank nearly missed the second site because they were so deep in conversation. The sky was its usual breathless white-blue, the sea a dark perfect royal and the sun cut the cliff shadows in cuneiform slashes, only revealing their depth when seen sideways.

By the time they returned, Audrey was tired, dozing in the cart. Hank took all her gear himself, shooing her off to nap. He rinsed and stacked their wetsuits, booties and BCEs in a thoughtful silence. The tanks to be filled, swapped, the dives logged on the computer — all his usual tasks were done while watching the colors of the hills.

He was pulling on his shirt to drive home when a thought struck him. *What if I had to work in an office? What if I worked at one of those tourist places, in a bar or a restaurant? On my feet all day being yelled at? What if Khaled made me run one of his electronics places in Cairo? Selling stolen goods and living in some dark little apartment? Dirty air and dirty money.*

He studied the idea on the ride back. Thought about it as he made his dinner. He imagined working in the US, doing what exactly? Managing...computers? The idea turned his stomach, so singularly appalling. Winter coats and rednecks, violence and no healthcare. Some trailer in the flatlands, water he could only dive in three months a year? He ate his dinner on the balcony, watching the market fill with people, the lanterns coming on in strings up and down the seaside street.

My head was so far up my ass. Sure, I can't think my own thoughts before I pay Khaled back. But because of Samir, I ain't got big men with bats at my door every week. I'm paying the loan without my knees getting broken. I have a nice place. I own that little plot off the road. I work six hours a day, tops. And I dive. I get paid to dive. To take people like Audrey and change their lives.

It was too much to think about before bed. But when he pulled the blankets up and punched his pillow into shape, it occurred to him that Cole, observant, intuitive

Cole, had understood. He had seen Hank's world, identified it as a paradise to be envied, and Hank had missed that. Had missed it completely.

The tension in his shoulders loosened a little, the grip around his heart letting go enough for him to let out a long, slow sigh. His last thought as he fell asleep was *Cole was right. I already have everything else. All I was missing was him. And I blew it.*

Hank was woken up by banging on his door and Leila's voice on the other side, laughing with someone between bangs.

Even for a Copt in her sixties, a woman barging into a single man's apartment simply wasn't done. So Hank shouted to her to wait a moment and made sure he was fully dressed and the front room tidied before opening the door. He wasn't an animal.

He needn't have worried. There was a veritable crowd in the hall. Not only Leila, but Fatima, Fatima's son, Dr. Faroud, Nader, even Samir, looking exceedingly grumpy to have been dragged up at this hour. Which—what time was it, anyway?

"It is seven in the morning, and you must be ready to leave by eight," Fatima said as Hank escorted her to the best chair. "Boy, make the coffee!"

Her son trotted off to the kitchen. When Hank protested, Leila swatted at him.

"Get the Horus," she said. "And be quick about it."

"Shit." The words slipped out, and he was enveloped in a chorus of chiding grandmothers. There was no arguing with them. Dr. Faroud was practically bouncing on his toes.

The tub on the table, Hank stepped back. He took a cup from Fatima's son and stood by Samir.

"What is this all about?"

"We have decided to help you," Samir said. "They came to me last night. If it is true—if this is all real? It will save us. It will save the Grande. Your debt will be paid in no time at all. You should have come to me."

"I'm sorry, Sam," Hank said quietly. "I truly am. I've been a real fool, you know? I should never have gotten so far in my own head."

"This is true. And what of the American? We must get him back for you."

"You know I can't."

"Don't be stupid!" Leila cried, overhearing them. "Hank, you are being very stupid. Everyone in the town knows you are not going to suddenly marry some local girl. We know. We all know. And no one cares. You are a good man. You were happy. And we all want our Hank to be happy."

"Damn," Hank said. He couldn't peel his eyes off the floor, overcome with emotion. The prickling in his eyes, the sudden construction in his chest—what could he say? *Nothing.*

"We are your people, Hank," Fatima said, banging her cane on the floor with a sharp rap. "Who else will stand for you?"

"You tended me when I was hurt."

"You are the only reason I still have clients at the dive shop."

"You helped me build my kiln."

"You helped my son pass his exams."

"This is real."

They all stopped and turned to Dr. Faroud. The old archeologist knelt on the floor in front of the low table. The open tub with its smelly water was off to the side, the falcon dripping in Dr. Faroud's hands. His hand lens swung on its chain around his neck as he looked at them each in turn, solemn as an owl.

"It is real, my friends," he repeated.

There was a silence in which they all looked at one another. The implications filled the room. Archeologists, camera crews, dive teams, tourists—all coming. All coming to their sleepy, half-forgotten town.

"Hamdullilah," Fatima whispered. "Alhamdullilah..."

"Shukran lak minal-a'maaq," Samir added. "Hank. You must go to Cairo. You must go now."

"My son will drive you," Fatima said.

"The party is tonight," Leila added. She looked at her watch. "We have time, but he must leave soon."

"What party?" Hank's mind flailed between the falcon in Dr. Faroud's hand, the relief that the decision had been taken from him and confusion at what was obviously a plan by the others.

"Do you own a suit?"

"What? Why?"

"I thought not, so I brought one," Samir said. "We are close enough that it will fit you."

"Wait," Hank said, holding out his hands to all of them. "What is happening here?"

"The American Embassy is hosting an exhibit. It opens tonight. It's at the Luxoria Hotel in Cairo. Everyone in the ancient art world will be there...including Cole and the Minister of Antiquities."

"You will go, and take the Horus," Dr. Faroud said. "We will wrap it for you."

"Give the Horus to Cole," Fatima said. "He will know what to do. He will make sure they take us seriously. Look." She pulled a clipped newspaper out of her purse. When she opened it, her lips curled in a smile. "He is such a good boy."

It was an article taken from Cole's writing. Hank read it even as the others began to gather what he would need, Dr. Faroud loudly insisting someone take him to the site immediately, that he be taught to dive this very day. The impassioned plea in the article, the absolute belief in the sovereignty of a country over its own history... Hank's breath hitched in his chest. Of course Cole had been shocked. Selling the Horus would have been counter to everything he believed. And Hank agreed. Wasn't he himself working at the Grande exactly to *avoid* getting into that kind of thing?

Faster than Hank would have thought possible, he was bundled into Fatima's ancient Toyota, her son at the wheel, the Horus wrapped in a blanket and packed in a bag at his feet. Samir's suit and a packed lunch were in the back, as well as a backpack with spare clothes. They all gathered in the parking lot and waved in the rearview until a curve in the road took them beyond view.

They drove for more than an hour before the entire situation came clear in his mind. He was on his way to see Cole! The Horus was real. The entire sordid question was solved, and Hank was on the right side.

Cole will know I did the right thing. He won't think of me as a thief. No matter what happens. And I'll tell him how different things are now, how much better I feel. That he made all the difference for me.

Chapter Twenty-One

Cole

The new antiquities minister was much nicer than the old one. Since the merge with the ministry of tourism, there had been some jockeying for position, but Dr. Adnan Al-Amah was settled in his role now. As soon as it was clear the new American ambassador was on his side about repatriation, he had become good friends with Leon, the cultural attaché, and so also with Cole.

While Cole was generally concerned with modern Egyptian art, Dr Adnan appreciated his support, and Cole enjoyed listening to Dr Adnan's stories of catching grave robbers in the nineteen-eighties and nineties. More importantly, Cole had become good friends with one of Dr. Adnan's aides. And she was the one he planned to discuss the site in Al'Shahin, what he had seen, and what she thought he should do about it.

"This is extraordinary," Yasmine said. "I see what you mean." They had moved out of the main gallery area and into an alcove with a table and chairs. An intimate space away from the voices and music of the main party. Cole, knowing the way these events worked, had ensured there were several of these out-of-the-way places. Not only for the more sensitive of his artists to take a break, but for deals to be struck, work to be purchased and the chance for the artists to mingle and be heard away from those who were just here to be seen.

"It was only visible for that hour," Cole said, pointing to the tumble of blocks in the photo. He had laid them out in order, viewed as a dive descended. "The light was shining from both sides, bouncing off the cliff face. The day before, none of this was obvious."

"And you say there were artifacts?"

"I'm not sure," Cole hedged. "But there was such a jumble of rocks. It seems like the whole cliff face gave way."

"These are sections of column," Yasmine said, turning the photo sideways. "Here and here. The shape of them — of course it is impossible to tell — but they are stacks of discs, rather than bricks, and that concerns me."

"Concerns you?"

She gave him a radiant smile and shook the photos under his nose. "Concerns me that they might be really old. Which means a big discovery and a very busy summer for me!"

"The divemaster thought they were columns too," Cole said. He bit back the bitterness in his voice. This moment of triumph wasn't the time to air out his heartbreak. *He's supposed to be here. Supposed to be by my side. I should be showing him off to everyone. This is his moment too.*

"Good," Yasmine said briskly. "We will need his expertise. There will be coordination between the environmental ministry too, since the coral reefs are protected. *Tch!* It will be bureaucratic madness until we can pin down who is in charge."

"Oh, how long will that delay the exploration of the site?"

"Not at all." She laughed. "The archeologists from University of Cairo will be on you like flies on honey. I hope Al'Shahin is ready for the influx!"

"They are," Cole said. "And frankly, they could use the boost."

"I know." Yasmine sighed. "It's been a tough few years. But this will be very good for them."

Cole swallowed around the sudden lump in his throat. *Good for them, yes. The artists, the dive operators, the hotels and restaurants. Hank will get his debt paid in no time. God, I wish I'd stayed and talked to him. I could have helped him. Shown a little fucking compassion. Big Hank, sweet, careful, big-hearted Hank. God I miss him. Helped me find my muse.*

Cole's apartment, once no more than a plain box, was a riot of color. Every spare moment was spent drawing and painting. Oils as he'd predicted, the ocean and mountains and sky covering every available surface. And under a casually thrown drop cloth, a smile, shy and mischievous, hazel eyes, firelight—Hank.

He only half-listened as Yasmine began to draw on some of his photos, indicating shapes even beyond what Cole and Hank had discovered. *Hank should be here. And if I hadn't gone so high and mighty, listened to him for just a minute. He'd be here. He'd be the man of the hour. I have to go back.*

Go back. *Go back!* The idea had not even occurred to him. But of course that was stupid. He could go back tomorrow. He could call Hank tonight. Right now even.

"Yasmine," Cole said. "I'm sorry, afwan, I just realized that I need to call that divemaster. Like, now. I made a huge mistake."

Yasmine tucked a stray hair into her hijab, pencil tapping on the paper.

"Cole Hadley," she said. "What are you talking about? Why are you blushing like that? You know what? I don't care. Your call can wait five minutes. I texted Adnan and he is coming over already."

Cole deflated. She was right of course. Five minutes wouldn't make that big of a difference. What mattered was Cole was not going to let Hank go that easily.

Hank watched Cole talking to the young woman for a moment, his feet frozen to the floor. Had he forgotten how handsome Cole was? Even in a suit... No. Especially in a suit. Cole was self-assured. He knew who he was and was sure of his own worth. It was the same confidence he had shown with the artists in Al'Shahin. Hank tugged the hem of his jacket. The bag with the Horus was digging into his shoulder. Cole's face was animated, but he looked drawn, tired. Guilt twisted Hank's belly. Was that his fault? Probably. Cole looked like he needed a good meal and a long sleep.

That idea spurred Hank forward. No matter what, even if Cole told him to fuck off, returning the Horus was the right thing to do. It would show Cole how much he had influenced Hank's life. He could at least know Hank had heard him, believed him, knew he was right. *I'm not some asshole stealing stuff. I'm not that guy. If all he knows is that — then that matters.*

He hurried through the throng, catching glimpses of the art out of the corner of his eye, but focused only on Cole. The woman with him was looking at photos. Cole's photos. Hank knew without seeing that Leila was right—Cole had waited until tonight to tell someone about the site.

"Cole," he called, weaving through. "Cole!"

"*Hank?*" Cole took a step forward, face blazing with astonished joy.

"Hey, hello, uh, hi." Hank shoved the flapping wings in his belly to the side, his eyes drinking in Cole's face.

"What are you doing here?"

"I brought..." Words Hank had rehearsed a thousand times in the car slipped away. He was caught by Cole's eyes, his expression—happiness quickly suppressed under suspicion. But the happiness had been there. He hadn't imagined it. Had he? Mute, Hank held up the bag.

"What is this?" the woman asked. Her voice was low and musical, expression amused. Hank and Cole stood frozen, staring at each other. Thank God, Cole recovered first. Hank didn't think he could speak if he tried.

"Yasmine, this is Hank Ashton. Hank is the divemaster from Al'Shahin who found the site."

"Pleasure to meet you," Yasmine said. "You are going to be quite famous, Mr. Ashton."

"Thank you, ma'am," Hank said, dragging his eyes away from Cole's. "I brought—we found something. At the site. I brought it. I mean." He looked back to Cole who was staring at the bag, eyebrows climbing his forehead.

"You *brought* it?"

"Yeah, I never, well, you know. I didn't do that. I couldn't. You were right. You were right about everything." Hank knew he was babbling, but he couldn't stop. "I was really blind. I should have seen what you were trying to show me. I want you to know —"

"Not here," Cole snapped. But his eyes were swimming with tears. "Not here," he repeated, more softly. "One thing at a time."

Again there was a whirlwind of activity around Hank. They moved to another room. The ambassador was there, and the Minister of Antiquities. A couple of artists.

Hank unwrapped the Horus carefully. "We kept it in water at first, but Dr. Faroud —"

"Hamed Faroud?"

"Yes. He wrapped it and told me to being it."

"You should have left it in the sea," the minister said, glaring suspiciously.

"We didn't think it was real, sir," Cole said. "Truly. I didn't even think it was real gold until we had it on the boat."

The minister seemed mollified. Everyone leaned forward as the last of the wrappings were eased away. Hank stepped back, placing himself beside Cole, his heart hammering away.

"Dr. Faroud said it was real," he murmured so only Cole could hear.

It was quiet while the people around the table leaned in, turning and passing the Horus from hand to hand. They replaced it on its blanket and an instant argument broke out. Rapid-fire Arabic from the archeologists, Yasmine showing the photos — Cole, Hank and even Ambassador Jenks were totally forgotten.

"You're getting a promotion for this even if I have to draw it up myself," Ambassador Jenks said, gripping Cole by the shoulder. "And you, Mr. Ashton. What's your story?"

"Hank is a Navy veteran and the best divemaster on the Red Sea," Cole said. "If there is any role for Uncle Sam in this — " He gestured to the Egyptians. "Then Hank should lead a dive team. The discovery is his."

Dr. Al-Amah came over, his face shining with excitement. "My dear friends," he said. "This is spectacular. I will let these gentlemen argue about which era it is from, but they agree it is real. It is ancient. I am going to approach the government Monday morning for funding to explore the site."

Hank let out a ragged sigh of relief. He felt light, delighted. A burden lifted from him. Cole was beaming, which was all Hank cared about. Ambassador Jenks was no fool. He saw his chance.

"I'm going to call my team in Washington as well," he said. "National Geographic, anyone we can get to assist in this. Funding included. You tell me what you need, Adnan, and I will fight for it."

Dr. Al-Amah rubbed his hands together. "The English will be very annoyed with us."

"Good," Ambassador Jenks said. "I can't wait to tell Lord Fawlter." He turned to the two men. "Cole, if you want, you can go home. I don't think the regular party events are going to happen now. Word is already spreading. I see Dr. Raman coming this way, and Dr. Bernam. I'll make sure things are taken care of here."

"Thank you, sir," Cole said. Hank looked at him. Cole's voice was tight, face stiff. "Come on, Mr. Ashton. Let's go get something to eat."

Chapter Twenty-Two

Cole

Cole's heart was beating so loudly he was sure Hank must be able to hear it. They walked in silence, Cole navigating without thought to his favorite restaurant in the neighborhood. It was small and busy. More importantly the men who ran it were friends. They had helped Cole with his Arabic when he first moved to the area.

"Okay," Cole said, as they settled at a tiny table in the corner. They ordered a plate of kushari and tea — no sense in getting fancy. The restaurant was hopping, which meant Hank and Cole could shout their secrets and no one would even notice. "Tell me the whole story."

Hank twisted his fingers together, his eyes on the table, his face drawn down in his grumpy grouper mode. Cole looked away to keep from smiling.

"You left," Hank said. "And I didn't do anything for a few days. I was... It was bad. I was so angry. But also — damn it, Cole, I knew you were right. I knew you were right, and it killed me."

"Is this an apology?" Cole asked. Hank sounded more angry than apologetic, and Cole was not prepared to let him get away with that.

"I'm gettin' to that," Hank said. "I had to come to my senses first. I realized right away that with you gone — well, I was real miserable. That was obvious. I missed you. I missed you way more than I should have."

"What the hell?"

"What I mean is — " Hank looked up, and Cole sucked in a breath. Hank's expression was all pain and misery. "You an' me, we didn't spend that much time together. But you left and it felt like someone tore a hole in my life. I can't believe how far under my skin you got. In...what — ten days?"

"Me too," Cole blurted. He sighed in frustration. But he had never been good about hiding his feelings. "Everyone said I was crazy to miss you so much when we barely spent any time together."

Their dish came, rice and lentils and vegetables, sizzling hot with a pile of pita. They didn't even bother with individual plates, just leaned over and dug in. Cole realized he was starving. When had he last eaten? Breakfast? Maybe? His old anxieties about eating in front of other people floated up. Until Hank held out a spoonful, and Cole took it without thought. Again. His tongue on the spoon made him shiver, catching Hank's twinkling eyes.

"I was gonna ask if you thought that was okra," he said.

Cole closed his eyes to chew — yes, okra, mixed in with the stewed tomatoes. "Maybe eggplant too?" he said, opening his eyes again.

"I never called anyone about the falcon," Hank said. "I just...went back to work. Went back to my life. Same as always." The table creaked as Hank leaned forward, his expression intent. "But nothing was the same, Cole. Nothing at all. Everything you saw, I saw. The colors, the people, every little thing I had been ignoring."

Hank leaned back in his chair, studying Cole, drumming his fingers on the table. Cole was sorely tempted to blurt out some other compromising nonsense. He clamped his teeth shut around the traitorous words crowding up his throat. *You look good. The sound of your voice is making my toes curl. I already feel better than I have since I left — just sitting here with you. I've been staring at your picture like a goddamn idiot.* None of that was escaping his clenched jaw. Nope. He took another mouthful of food to shut them up.

"You look rough, baby," Hank said, his voice gentle. "Ain't nobody take care of you here?"

"No." The word popped like a bubble straight from the churning in Cole's gut. How had Hank darted around his defenses and straight to the cut like that? Well, Cole didn't need anyone to take care of him, did he? *Of course I do. Everyone does. That's exactly the problem, right?*

"Look," Cole said, fighting for any semblance of perspective. "I've missed you. You really hurt me. And I really hurt you. But it was just... We didn't understand each other. And the falcon — you brought it here. You... I want to say I knew you would do the right thing. But I didn't know. You never told me any of the things keeping you in Al'Shahin. I just want to ask one thing. Do you regret it? Our time together?"

Hank crossed his arms, but then uncrossed them, laying his hands flat on the table.

"I don't regret *nothing*," he said hotly. "Not a goddamn thing. I don't care if you send me back to the coast and never speak to me again." He leaned forward again, his eyes intent. "You changed my life, Cole. I see things different. I feel like a new man. So no matter what, it was worth it. Every second with you was worth it."

Cole absorbed this, taking slow bites of their food. They had already destroyed half the plate — their nerves clearly translating into hunger. Cole felt less shaky. A long swallow of tea, minty fresh, helped clear his thoughts further. Pretending was bullshit. Denying his feelings was too, and new Cole was not going to self-sabotage this.

"I want to take you back to my place."

Hank almost flipped the table standing up. The last knot in Cole's chest gave way, and he laughed, a joyful release of sound even as he saved the rattling teapot. Hank grinned down at him, his sun-lined face exactly matching Cole's mood.

"Come on," Hank said, throwing bills onto the table. "Let me show you how much I missed you."

* * * *

The door to Cole's apartment slammed under his back. He didn't give Hank a second to catch his breath, kissing him, tasting their dinner and mint tea. When Hank tried to pull back, exclaiming at the art on every surface, half-finished paintings and sketches, Cole nipped his lower lip.

"Tomorrow, Hank," he said, trying to undo both their buttons at once. "God, you look good in a suit, too. That isn't fair."

Hank replied by slapping Cole's hands away, scrambling out of his shirt and jacket even as he pushed his face into Cole's neck. "Okay, tomorrow, baby. Goddamn I want you so bad. Been thinking about this every day."

"Me too," Cole said, his voice choked as Hank lapped at the skin under his ear. They nearly fell, twice, leaving a trail of clothes from the door to the bed, which to be fair, wasn't very far.

Hank fell back onto the bed, pulling Cole on top of him. When Cole tried to lift himself up, take some of the weight off, Hank bit him and yanked him down again.

"Want every part of you." He gripped Cole's neck, holding them eye to eye. "Every. Fucking part of you." Then he winked and bucked his hips up so their cocks ground together. "Especially that part."

"Well in that case…"

* * * *

Cole kept his eyes closed, despite the shaft of morning light on his face. He was alone in his bed, but that didn't concern him. The ache in his hips, the scent of Hank on the pillow, even the way the blankets were carefully tucked around him — it wasn't a dream.

If that wasn't enough, he could hear his lover rattling around the little kitchen, and smell coffee over even the sweet musk of sex in his bed. Hank was humming to himself, and Cole listened a moment in perfect happiness before turning over and levering himself up.

The joy of a tiny apartment? He could sit up in bed, propped on his pillows, and see Hank in the kitchen.

Hank was in a pair of jeans and an old T-shirt, worn and thin and criminally tight over his big shoulders. The tiny table by the window was piled with food. Cole recognized the box from his local pastry shop, but there was also a colorful bowl of fruit salad and, oh blessed — a big pot of coffee.

Hank was doing dishes, and as much as Cole wanted to run over and hug that big back, he let the moment fill him. *This is what it will be like. This is what he meant by taking care. The big lug got up and bought all that stuff just to have a nice breakfast for me. This could be exactly what it's like when we are together — waking up with him, going to sleep with him. Making him laugh.*

An urge to paint came over him. A quiet domestic scene, Dutch Masters style, *Man Making Breakfast for His Lover.*

That made him laugh, and Hank turned, face lighting up.

"Hey, sleepyhead," he said. "I was about to drink all this coffee myself."

"Terrible man. Cruel, terrible man!"

Cole clambered out of the bed. He reached for a shirt, then saw the way Hank was smirking and straightened.

"Like what you see?"

"Yes," Hank said. His voice was a low rumble, his expression more shark than grouper. Butterflies took off in Cole's stomach.

"You'll excuse me if I put on clothes anyway," he said. "You can undress me with your eyes better that way."

"I look forward to it," Hank replied. "And yes to coffee. Made it just how you like."

"What a man." Cole laughed, pulling on a shirt and briefs. That was enough. The novelty of being ogled wasn't likely to wear off anytime soon.

They ate in silence for a time, except for Cole complimenting the food. In addition to beautiful croissants from the local French place, Hank had made eggs, fluffy and spicy enough to make Cole's eyes water. The coffee was strong. The fruit salad was cold and seasoned with vanilla and lemon. It was the best breakfast Cole had had in a long time.

"I could get used to this," Cole said around a mouthful of croissant dipped in coffee.

"Good," Hank said. He leaned back, his face warm and relaxed. "I have to head back to Al'Shahin. Everyone is dying to know what happened with the Horus. But I'll be seeing you soon. yeah?"

"God yes. You'll never get rid of me now," Cole said with a smile. He took Hank's hand, pressed his lips to the scarred knuckles.

"Good," Hank said. He came around and cupped Cole's face. "You came and kicked me right out of my rut, Cole. I'm gonna be good to you. I'm gonna pay off my debt with the diving we'll do for the Horus. Then I'll open my own shop. You'll have a gallery, and we will tear up the road between Cairo and Al'Shahin."

"About that," Cole said. "I hope you know, I plan to push hard for a posting in Al'Shahin while the work is being done."

"That's even better."

Their kiss goodbye couldn't drag too long—Fatima's son needed to get back with the car. But it didn't matter. However long it took to sort out Cole's assignments, Hank's debts, the politics of the site—none of that mattered. They had everything they needed now.

Chapter Twenty-Three

Hank

Hank had a whole new life. Every morning he rose before dawn and had his coffee on his balcony, honoring the beauty Cole had shown him, a self-imposed observance he refused to rush. When his gratitude, and the sun, had risen high enough, he could head to the hotel for his first batch of students. Who, it turned out, were lovely people, of course. *Now that I ain't an asshole. Now that I see.*

The classes were filling up, young people eager to learn. It turned out his former students, the kids from Tel Aviv, had some sort of internet thing. Hank didn't understand—influence over what exactly? But pictures of him were apparently all over, and the girls had *blown him up*—which sounded ominous but Mariam, the blonde, assured him it was good. It seemed like half of Tel Aviv University came through the Grande on long weekends now.

"Thank you, Cole," he said, trailing his arm out of the truck window.

"For what? Oh God, not green, Leon! Nothing before the seventeen-hundreds was that shade of —" Cole's voice was distracted, despite the fact that he insisted on calling Hank every morning.

Hank didn't answer, let Cole's laughing argument with his boss carry him from truck to dive shop. *I love you, Cole Hadley. I love you.* He wasn't ready to say it out loud yet. But it was there. And Hank had the glorious conviction that Cole was thinking it too.

Things moved faster than Hank would have believed, caught as he had been in the sleepy Groundhog Day life of a tourist town. The Antiquities Department sent a crew of divers, but not nearly enough for the task, and as a result Al'Shahin was suddenly inundated with foreigners as well as archeologists and scientists.

Hank, not wanting to miss out, pulled double shifts, working at the Grande to pay his debt and then high tailing it out to the site to lead more technical dives there. It was exhausting, but Hank loved it. Especially when the dive experts started pouring in — there were happy reunions left and right.

Happy yes, but by the end of each day he was shattered, listening to Cole's warm voice, wrapped in his blanket.

"How much longer until you're here, baby?"

"A week. And I hope you're ready for what's coming."

"You got no idea. The place is already filling up. Divers from all over are on their way. Including one of my best friends." Hank yawned. "Lucky as hell to get him. Name is Levi Cunningham."

"Sounds familiar," Cole said, glancing up from his canvas. Watching him paint helped Hank fall asleep. The teddy bear had a dab of paint on his nose, and

Hank felt a happiness so acute he had to close his eyes. "How do I know that name?"

"He was all over the news last year. Saved those little kids stuck in a flooded cave in Malaysia?"

"Oh my God! I remember that! What the hell is he doing there?"

"He's the best person for moving stone—if we don't want the rest of that cliff down on us."

"Damnit, I don't want to miss that! But I still have a week here!"

"Better get a move on, baby," Hank said. "You're gonna—" He was interrupted by his own yawn, his body a slow throb of exhaustion.

"Hey." Cole turned to the camera, the dab of paint on his nose now joined by another on his forehead. "Don't work too hard. I need my man functioning when I get there!"

My man, he says. Just says it so casual. I love you, Cole. I really do. I can't wait to say it.

"I still gotta work down my debt, baby. I'm down to about seven thousand," Hank mumbled, his phone propped up where he could see it. "And no one has seen Khaled for weeks."

"I wish you would let me loan you the money," Cole said. He was exasperated, his round face trying to scowl. But scowling wasn't Cole's ability. Especially not with paint on his nose. That was Hank's superpower.

"Don't make that grumpy grouper face at me, Hank Ashton." Cole laughed. "I just hope you know it's a serious offer!"

"Listen," Hank countered. "Then I would just owe *you* money. And I'm too old and feeble to be your sex slave."

Cole's laughter filled the room. "Go to sleep, sailor," he said. "I'm gonna shower and do the same."

* * * *

Sleep, sunrise vigil, classes with laughing cohorts of students, food eaten as he drove pell-mell up the coast, team meetings, map and geology consults, dive, dive, dive into the evening. Eat, call Cole, and sleep again. Every day was a marathon and every day brought something new and wonderful.

"Hank Ashton!"

"Levi?" Hank snapped out of his stupor and blinked into the setting sun. The figure approaching him was unmistakable, though. Levi "Tanks" Cunningham and his tech team had arrived. Hank clambered to his feet, his exhaustion forgotten. Levi grabbed him in a bear hug, despite his head barely reaching Hank's chin, curly blond and threaded through with gray now. When had they all grown so old?

"Dang, son! You look good!" Hank held Levi at arm's length. Smiling, scruffy round face and green eyes, shaped exactly like a block of cement Levi fucking Cunningham! "How the hell did they manage to get you for this?"

"When I read your name on that presser, I thought I'd lost my mind," Levi said. His freckled face wreathed in smiles. "I said, what the hell is Henry Ashton doing in Al'Shahin! I jumped at the chance. I'm going to move those rocks for you. But not for a few days. I want to know everything you been doing since Thailand."

"Boy, have I got a story to tell you," Hank laughed. "I been dying to talk to you, but you have no phone! Come and have dinner."

"Aw sorry, man." Levi didn't sound the slightest bit upset. He fell in besides Hank with his usual side-to-side sailor's roll. "I lost my phone somewhere in Malaysia. Forgot to get another one. You cooking? Hell yes, I wouldn't turn down your food for anything."

"Bring the whole gang," Hank said. "And I want to hear about you, too. National hero of Malaysia? Is it true *National Geographic* gave you a cover? Can I have your autograph?"

It was easy to tease Levi. He didn't have an egotistical bone in his body and believed the best of everyone. Sure enough, he took Hank's arm, green eyes blazing.

"I'm not a hero, Hank," he said. "You'd have done the same thing. The only thing the rescue team needed was someone to navigate the tunnel and move the rocks."

"Bullshit." Hank shook Levi's shoulder, even as he pulled open the door to the truck. "You're the most respected cave diver in the world. Of course they called you to save those kids. You deserve every bit of credit."

"They were so little," Levi said, and Hank looked closer, saw the troubled look in Levi's round face. "And...and we lost one, you know." How could Hank forget? He curled his arm around Levi's shoulders and ushered him into the truck. It sounded like they all had things they needed to sort out.

"Hey. Come to dinner. Tell me all about it. I'll tell you about my boyfriend and how this whole mess went down."

"Boyfriend?"

"You'll meet him next week. Now come on. I have lamb kebobs marinating..."

* * * *

Cole

Cole landed in Al'Shahin two months to the day of his first arrival. Stepping out of the tarmac glare and into the bustling airport, the first thing he saw was Hank, holding a bouquet of flowers. *Oh God, look at him. Look how happy he is. Tired though. I gotta keep him from working too hard.*

They didn't kiss at the airport or hold hands, but Hank nearly frog marched him to the truck, and they made it less than a mile before Hank screeched onto a wide road shoulder and yanked Cole into his arms. He smelled like salt and sweat and roasting spices, and Cole wondered again, physiologically, if it was possible to be so happy. Could a heart really burst? It sure felt like it.

"Hank, my grumpy grouper. I missed you."

"It's only been six weeks!" Hank laughed, then leaned in and nipped Cole's lip. "But say it again. Say it a million times 'cause I missed you too, teddy bear. Please tell me all those cases and boxes in the back mean you're staying for a bit?"

Glancing over his shoulder at the full truck bed, Cole gave a firm nod.

"I am here for the haul," Cole said. Hank's jaw drop was worth it. "I rented the apartment next to yours. The little studio."

"That was you?" Hank cried. "That's perfect! Oh my God, Imma cut a door between us!"

"Already organized, sailor boy."

"Well damn. I was gonna offer my place, since the Grande is full," Hank said shyly, rubbing the back of his neck.

"There's a feast in your honor tonight," Hank warned, squeezing Cole hard and plastering his face with loud smacking kisses. "I hope you're ready for the madness."

"Who's coming?"

"Everybody," Hank said, "every single person you can imagine."

* * * *

The feast was as promised, fully half the town assembled on Leila's beautiful terrace, celebrating not only their newest neighbor, but Horus, the site and the life of their town.

Cole was greeted by a gaggle of people, most of whom he recognized. Fatima, her apprentice and the whole women's collective, Samir from the Grande, Nader and the other stone carvers, Hank's students, Dr. Faroud, with a circle of young archeologists from the university—and they all burst into cheers when he reached the patio.

A *Welcome Back, Cole!* banner hung between the orange trees, bobbing among the lanterns festooning their branches.

Cole stopped in amazement, steadied by Hank's wide hand on his back. The smell of woodsmoke and roasting food enveloped him as much as the greetings of all their friends. He took one deep swirling breath, and dove into the crowd.

"This is beautiful," Cole said, once he had cleared the initial scrum and settled on a chair beside Fatima and Samir. They were all balancing plates of food, flatbreads and Hank's flaky fish and endless lamb in tomatoes and okra.

"Is it true you have taken the place beside Hank?" Sam asked, leaning forward and swirling his bread into the lemony sauce.

"Yes," Cole said around a mouthful of fish. "I'll telework to Cairo three days a week, but my primary responsibility is being a liaison to the site."

"I bet they give you whatever you want," Hank said, dropping in with glasses of iced melon juice and mint. "You're famous now."

"Not as famous as you!" Sam slapped Hank on the shoulder. "This one is the talk of the Sea. Hank the Hunk they call him now!"

"Them kids," Hank said with a groan. "They put me all over the internet."

"Please," Cole snorted. "Who do you think made that profile? Mariam and I have a whole Hank fandom to manage."

"It's fabulous publicity," Sam said, gripping Cole's arm. "You would not believe the way our website traffic has grown."

"You should have seen the dispatch. *Navy Veteran dedicated to Egyptian sovereignty* — it was very patriotic. If he doesn't score a Nat Geo gig after this, I'll eat my fins."

"Speaking of Nat Geo," Hank called over his shoulder, "here comes their starboy."

"Did I hear y'all talking about me?" came a new voice. A stocky blond man in a Hawaiian shirt ambled up and rubbed Hank's bald head. He grinned at seeing Cole and held out his hand. "Oh hey, you must be Cole. Nice to meet you. I'm Levi."

"Hey," Cole said, fighting back a smile. Levi Cunningham looked absolutely nothing like he'd imagined. The cave diver was a stocky white guy with sun-bleached curly hair and a round, earnest face. *He looks like the plucky stoner character in a movie. In a trucker hat. Is he wearing Crocs? Of course he is. Oh my God. I love him.*

"Well, what did you expect?" Hank asked with a laugh when Cole pulled him aside.

"I dunno," Cole said. "Someone more...heroic, I guess. Instead he's the cutest little surfer dude in Crocs."

"Don't worry. He's a monster when it comes to the job. He'll get your palace uncovered without anyone so much as stubbing a toe. Now you come with me a second. Let's catch our breaths."

They went around to the front of the terrace, looking up at the stars. Cole leaned back on Hank's chest, warm in the circle of his arms. They swayed in silence a moment, cheeks pressed, letting the moment settle. It was real. They were here, between the Sahara and the Sea. Together.

"I paid off my debt," Hank said softly. "I been meaning to tell you. Sam paid Khaled and warned him off. Says he's left for Asia anyway. But no matter what, I'm free and clear."

"Oh, Hank," Cole said, dragging him down for a kiss. "You did it. All by yourself you did it."

"I couldn't have done it without you," Hank said, his hands warm and rough cupping Cole's cheeks. "I love you, Cole."

"Hank..." Cole could barely speak. *He loves me. He loves me! He's good, and kind and takes care and he loves me.* His heart *had* burst, based on the firework bursts of joy exploding in his chest. "I love you too. I love you so much."

There was no more to say. They rejoined the others, fingers tangled, drifting in joy.

Want to see more like this?
Here's a taster for you to enjoy!

Intrinsic Values: Artifacts
Bailey Bradford

Excerpt

The *Help Wanted* sign in the window stopped Aldric in his tracks. He'd been walking along San Antonio's Pearl District, somewhat lost in his thoughts and worries, so why he noticed the sign, he couldn't have said.

Maybe because it stood out in the day of internet-everything. All the job boards that he'd scanned and the applications for employment that he'd sent in had been online. That was just how it was done nowadays…except not at the business he'd stopped in front of.

Aldric stared at the sign for a solid minute while trying to calculate his chances of being hired if he went in and applied before going home and changing. Not that he had any fancier clothes. Jeans, T-shirts and one button-up were all that was in his wardrobe.

What are the chances someone else will apply and get hired by the time I go home, shower, shave, change and come back?

Whatever the odds were, his empty stomach didn't want to risk them. Blinking away his musings, Aldric pushed his glasses farther up his nose, then caught himself screwing up his face to re-settle them exactly where they'd been. He attempted to smooth down his hair—being thick, it tended to tousle, even though it wasn't long—and reached for the door handle, which was when he saw the name of the place that was hiring.

Intrinsic Value Antique Shop. At least shop wasn't spelled all funky. It was a silly pet peeve he had, people adding extra letters onto words to make spellings like *shoppe* rather than shop. An antique store might have a better reason than most businesses or services to use an old spelling of the word, and he had no reason to be judgmental of anything—something he needed to keep in mind.

Even though he knew nothing about antiques, Aldric opened the door and stepped inside to the tinkling of chimes. He glanced down at the door handle inside and saw strings of silver and copper bells dangling from it.

"Good afternoon. May I help you?"

Aldric pivoted so quickly that he almost tripped over his own feet—nothing unusual for him. Heat rushed to his face, and he gulped as he spotted the older man standing with one hand on an ancient-looking cash register. "Er, yes, I, um, I—" Aldric took a deep breath and exhaled to the count of ten. If he didn't get himself calmed down, he'd stumble over his words as well as his feet, as he tended to do when he was flustered.

"My name is Elliot Douglas. I'm the owner of Intrinsic Value. Please call me Elliot." Elliot came around the counter and stopped in front of Aldric.

"Aldric Beamer." Aldric offered his right hand to shake. "Nice to meet you, Elliot." His mouth was dry, and a tickle started up in his throat.

"Nice to meet you, too." Elliot pumped his hand one more time, then let go. "Are you here about the job? I noticed you standing outside and thought you might be considering it."

Aldric covered his mouth and turned his head before he coughed. He lowered his hand and faced Elliot again. "Sorry, the mountain cedar is kicking my allergies into high gear. Yes, sir, I'm here about the job. Surprised me to see an actual sign in the window. Everything's done online, it seems. I've been told to go home and apply online so often, I've quit thinking about actual signs."

"Ah yes, the internet is an amazing tool for many things, but I prefer to meet people in person first, rather than online." Elliot smiled, and Aldric realized the older, taller man, with his tawny-brown eyes and thick mane of slightly long, wavy light-brown hair that was just starting to silver, was quite handsome.

"Why don't you come back this way and tell me what makes you think you'll be a good fit at Intrinsic Value?" Elliot gestured in the direction of the cash register. "I was cleaning off my baby and would like to finish as we talk."

"Yes, sir." Aldric coughed again and wanted to melt into the floorboards.

"Would you like some cold water or hot tea?" Elliot offered. "I have both available."

Aldric wasn't sure about hot tea. He'd only ever had Texas tea—cold, with lots of sugar and ice in it. But maybe tea was a thing with Elliot. "Er, tea, please?"

Elliot glanced back at him. "You sound uncertain. Have you tried hot tea before?"

Lying wasn't something Aldric did if he could help it. "I haven't, but I thought a warm drink might help with my scratchy throat."

"That it might. I have a few different kinds, but how about you try the chamomile? It's good for all sorts of ailments." Elliot stopped by an elegant-legged wooden table that had a silver tea kettle and several mismatched cups and saucers sitting on it.

A white ceramic dish held glass jars of tea and cubes of sugar, and a clear container was filled with what appeared to be honey. Delicate silver spoons were laid out as well. Aldric tucked his hands into the front pockets of his jeans. Everything on that table looked delicate, not only the spoons, and he was afraid to touch anything.

Which had to mean he shouldn't apply for the job.

"Aldric?" Elliot arched one thick eyebrow. "Is chamomile okay?"

Realizing he'd more than likely made sure he wouldn't get hired, because Elliot had to think he was on the dense side, Aldric shook his head. "It's okay, thank you. I'll just—" He started to take a step back.

"Just what?" Elliot asked, scooping tea from a jar before he put it into a little oval-shaped strainer. "Are you not interested in the job after all?"

Aldric bit his bottom lip and pondered whether he should stay or not. For one thing, he'd already made some kind of impression, good or bad. For another, Elliot hadn't run him off. *That has to mean I still have a chance, right? Until I tell him I know nothing about what this shop sells. Damn it.*

"I'm interested, but I don't have any experience with antiques," Aldric rushed out, watching Elliot pour hot water over the strainer holding the tea. Elliot had put a lid on it so the tea leaves didn't flow out.

Aldric took a step closer, unable to resist getting a better look at what Elliot was doing. He took off his round-framed glasses, polished them and shoved them back on.

"The tea needs to steep for a few minutes," Elliot explained. "The infuser keeps most of the bits of tea leaves from escaping, but you still might have a few pieces in your cup. Those will usually settle at the bottom."

"That's the infuser?" Aldric asked when Elliot nudged the strainer holding the tea.

Elliot smiled at him. "Yes, it is. Do you like honey?"

"I—" Aldric's stomach picked that moment to let out a rumbling growl. He dropped his gaze and pressed a fist to his belly. "Sorry. Skipped breakfast."

"Well, that won't do. It's almost time for dinner. I'll order us something to eat, then you and I will sit down for a proper interview—if you're interested in the job?" Elliot picked up the jar of honey.

"Oh, I...I am, I just thought I'd blown any chance I had at it." Aldric ducked his head and stared at the worn toes of his tennis shoes. "I don't have any experience for it. I've only worked at fast-food places. I don't know anything about antiques. I didn't even know what that thing—the infuser—was." His ignorance was embarrassing, and he hated that he didn't know more.

"So," Elliot drawled, one corner of his mouth curving up. "No experience at all? That would mean I'd have a clean slate in you, if I were to hire you. Wouldn't have to rid you of bad habits and misinformation."

Aldric was almost too afraid to believe he might have a chance of keeping his shitty apartment and not going hungry for much longer, after all. "Are you serious?"

About the Author

J Calamy is a queer, disabled veteran and foreign service wonk who spends a good part of the year bouncing down dirt roads in the back of range rovers with men with guns. Coffee, romance novels, and embassy scuttlebutt are her last remaining vices.

J Calamy loves to hear from readers. You can find her contact information, website details and author profile page at https://www.pride-publishing.com

PUBLISHING

Sign up for our newsletter and find out about all our romance book releases, eBook sales and promotions, sneak peeks and FREE romance books!